E-VIRUS

THE DIARY OF A MODERN DAY GIRL

Book 1
The Beginning of the End

Jessica was born in Lincolnshire, however she moved to Cheshire at the age of five. Jessica spent the majority of her childhood residing in Bramhall. She now lives in a lovely little apartment in Wilmslow, the area which inspired her first novel. Jessica works full-time as an Administration Manager for an aquatic science consultancy firm. In her spare time she enjoys traveling, shopping, going out with friends and tending to her adorable yet mischievous house bunny named Honey.

Jessica Ward

E-VIRUS

THE DIARY OF A MODERN DAY GIRL

Olympia Publishers
London

www.olympiapublishers.com
OLYMPIA PAPERBACK EDITION

Copyright ©Jessica Ward 2016
Cover by Nixxi Rose

The right of Jessica Ward to be identified as author of
this work has been asserted in accordance with sections 77 and 78 of the
Copyright, Designs and Patents Act 1988.

All Rights Reserved
No reproduction, copy or transmission of this publication
may be made without written permission.
No paragraph of this publication may be reproduced,
copied or transmitted save with the written permission of the publisher,
or in accordance with the provisions
of the Copyright Act 1956 (as amended).

Any person who commits any unauthorised act in relation to
this publication may be liable to criminal
prosecution and civil claims for damage.

A CIP catalogue record for this title is
available from the British Library.

ISBN: 978-1-84897-628-3

(Olympia Publishers is part of Ashwell Publishing Ltd)

This is a work of fiction.
Names, characters, places and incidents originate from the writer's
imagination. Any resemblance to actual persons, living or dead,
is purely coincidental.

Published in 2016

Olympia Publishers
60 Cannon Street
London
EC4N 6NP

Printed in Great Britain

For Lucy. Without your support none of this would be possible.

Acknowledgements

I would like to thank Nixxi Rose for graciously letting me use her fabulous designs for my front covers in this series. If you would like your very own hand-crafted zombie-skin products check out her online shop on Etsy!

https://www.etsy.com/uk/shop/NixxiRose

I would also like to thank all my family and friends who have supported me throughout and spread the word about my books.

Introduction

Ebola is a viral illness, in which symptoms include sudden fever, weakness, intense muscle pain, internal and external bleeding, redness of the eyes, vomiting, and diarrhoea and in most cases, death.

There is a twenty-one-day incubation period in which anyone who comes into close contact with the infected can contract the virus. For at least one of those weeks, carriers are not aware they are infected.

According to the World Health Organisation (WHO) Ebola first appeared in 1976 along the western coast of Africa. Two simultaneous outbreaks occurred in Sudan, Nzara and Yambuku, Demographic Republic of Congo, situated near the Ebola river, where the virus gets its name.

Ebola was first transmitted to humans through direct contact of infected animals, primarily fruit bats who are considered to be the natural hosts to the virus.

Ebola is transmitted through close contact via blood, secretions, organs and other bodily fluids.

There are currently no cures or vaccinations against the Ebola virus.

*

Think about how you feel when there's a power cut. What about when your water is switched off? Think about all those times your phone had no signal, or had run out of battery. Imagine your phone, laptop or tablet running out of battery and you had no way at all to charge it... ever.

How much work can you really get done when there's no Internet in your office? How far could you get if you didn't have your car, or if the transport links were cut off?

Now imagine all of the above, happening at the exact same time. What would you do? And how would you survive?

Nowadays people drive their cars to the gym, only to go inside and run on the spot on a treadmill, all the while watching the latest episode of EASTENDERS.

We do it because we can because we don't know any different.

Think about what we do at home. If we get peckish, we log onto the internet. We click a few buttons, and before you know it, all kinds of cuisine are delivered straight to our doors, twenty-four hours a day. Nowadays, even those that burn toast never go hungry.

I am no different to you. I relied massively on today's technology. Whether it be my iPhone (that never left my side), my iPad that allowed me to watch TV, stream movies and keep up with the latest gossip, even wake me up in the morning. Or my car that gave me complete freedom to go wherever the hell I want. I'll admit it; I still used the car when walking was a completely doable option.

In pretty much every single aspect of my life, I relied on all these things. I did it because it was there; I couldn't function without it.

You don't realise how much you take for granted, the simple things in life.

We rely so much on these things that, if they were to be taken away, then mankind simply cannot function.

This is my story. The story of how I had to survive the demise of the modern world, and witness the birth of a new, horrifying and deadly world in which there were no rules, no technology or comfort, and the infected walked among us.

The E-virus turned the whole world upside down. It left death and destruction in its wake. The only problem was: the dead didn't stay dead.

So let's go back to the beginning. What happened? How did it start? What makes my story different to any others?

Well, I'll tell you all about that. But as to what makes it different? Well, that's for you to decide. My story is different because it's what happened to me. Each person in this world has lived a different life to another. Circumstances, backgrounds and thought processes are different for each of us, and are what sets us apart from the rest. This might be like every other survival story you have ever heard, but I doubt it.

Chapter 1

The Outbreak

I first found out about the outbreak in its early stages. It was from a BBC news story, I remember it so clearly. I was sat in the office on a typical dull and dreary day swivelling on my chair, waiting for my next assignment to come in. The story was titled "Ebola Outbreak 'most challenging' as Guinea deaths pass 100".

The picture at the top of the page really drew my attention. Three people were carrying a stretcher covered with a plastic sheet. The people in the photo were all dressed in biohazard-type suits with aprons, turquoise Nitrile gloves and they had what looked like snorkel masks on. The outfits looked comical, but I found it quite worrying at the same time.

The article read like this:

> The number of people believed to have been killed by the Ebola virus in Guinea has passed one hundred, the UN World Health Organization says.

> It was "One of the most challenging Ebola outbreaks we have ever dealt with" And could take another four months to contain, the WHO said.
>
> The virus had now killed one hundred and one people in Guinea and ten in Liberia, it said.
>
> Ebola is spread by close contact and kills between 25% and 90% of its victims.
>
> Many West African states have porous borders, and people frequently travel between countries.
>
> Southern Guinea is at the epicentre of the outbreak, with the first case reported last month.
>
> The geographical spread of the outbreak is continuing to make it particularly challenging to contain – past outbreaks have involved much smaller areas.

My first thought was, this is happening miles away from me. It will never make its way over here. I'll be fine; this won't affect me. All the same, I was intrigued.

I read the whole article and soon after I found myself googling Ebola and the history behind it. I never knew it then, but the information I learnt would become invaluable to me in the future.

You're probably all thinking, what the hell does this girl do? Does she have nothing better to do all day then read pointless articles and google random health issues? Well, okay, that was a slow day. But before the outbreak I was just a normal girl, I had a good job and my focus was my career.

I worked for printing company dealing in food packaging; my job was to manage the Web advertising. I loved my job; not many people can say they spend all day on the likes of Facebook and get paid for it, but I could. Workwise I was going in the right direction. Since I started the Web sales shot up, and my work was even beginning to get noticed by the board of directors.

Like everyone else, it wasn't perfect. There was the office bitch in finance, the one who everyone hated. I'm sure you know the type. The busybody that should have spent more time getting her own job right, and less time criticising everyone else's. As you can imagine, I've had a few run-ins with her in my time.

Diane, the troll in question, was a particularly large woman, in her late forties. She had a face like a piranha and a personality to match. She was vile. Luckily for me, I didn't work in her department. Believe me, I felt for all those poor people who did. I had already encountered far too many staff members seeking refuge in the ladies toilets, wiping away the tears they had already shed that day. I was able to have minimal contact and avoid her where possible.

However, like most places, for each nasty, soul-sucking member of staff there you could also find their polar opposite. For me it was a sweet, bubbly and kind-hearted lady named Joyce. She was in her early sixties and had children around the same age as me. She had short mousey brown hair – the signs of grey were only just starting to creep up. She looked great for her age, she was always very active. Yoga was her new favourite hobby; she always told me how good it was for the mind. She had even invited me to a yoga retreat with her, but I had politely declined. I loved Joyce but yoga wasn't really my thing.

At twenty-five, I was one of the youngest in the office. Everyone was set in their ways and had been there for a great number of years. Joyce took me under her wing from my very first day. I felt I could confide in her about anything, and she would guide me in the right direction. Everyone needs a Joyce in their life.

So in terms of work, not only did I act the part, but I also made damn sure I looked it. I wore stiletto heels all day every day, seven days a week. In fact, I wore them that much I was only comfortable on my tiptoes. I could not, and would not wear flat shoes. I felt like I waddled; it was not a pretty sight.

I always made sure I was immaculately dressed both inside and outside of work; I lived out of my many pencil skirts and dresses.

I never left the house without my iPad, iPhone and Chanel Rouge lipstick, safety tucked inside my Hermes bag. I loved my designers; Selfridges was my second home. I knew my way around the Trafford Centre like the back of my hand. My friends often called me their personal shopping GPS, or PSGPS for short.

Like most people, I was fully dependent on technology. It's how everyone communicated. In those days, you were considered sociable just by sitting in a room trolling through Facebook. Social media ruled cyberspace. One picture taken at the Oscars was popular enough to crash Twitter. It was extremely powerful. Just like everyone else I had them all. I'm not ashamed to admit it, I Instagrammed my food whenever I visited fancy restaurants. I Snapchatted my morning brew. I even sent out LOLCATZ to my friends via e-mail during work hours.

In life, I was very independent. Everything I bought, I paid for myself. I was financially secure and, to me, it was the best feeling. Although I had a well-paid job and enjoyed the finer things in life, I took pride in the fact I was still very grounded.

Most of my friends were like me. They all lived in heels but they were very much into shopping, and all had their fair share of boys, and the drama that comes along with it. However, for as much as I looked the part, I didn't always share the same interests.

Yes, I could shop until I dropped, yet, I grew up on a farm in the country. I was very into my fast cars, shooting guns and jumping in puddles in my wellies. I loved adventure and I loved watching films so frightening that I wouldn't be able to sleep at night.

Back then I would have loved to have been part of a Zombie apocalypse. I watched every single zombie film I could get my hands on, I begged and begged my fiancé to take me on a zombie experience day. You know, the ones where you get transported to an abandoned shopping centre or abandoned building, and have to make your way through, whilst being attacked by various actors dressed like in the films. That was my idea of an unforgettable day out.

The reality is not as fun as I imagined it to be, that's for sure.

*

The outbreak started like any other, swine flu, avian flu, foot and mouth. You hear about it in the news, but precautions are put in place and eventually the media stories die down. This particular outbreak the Ebola virus started in the west coast of Africa. It was only a small story at first. Only a minute or two was dedicated to the stories of the Ebola outbreak and what was going on around us.

The world seemed to be more interested in the missing Malaysia Airlines plane and the war that seemed inevitable between Ukraine and Russia.

Only those who paid close attention from the beginning were truly aware of how fast the virus spread. Now I won't pretend to know how it started, it just happened. I started to get worried when I heard about how the countries around us were closing borders because of the virus. It seemed a bit drastic.

The various news sites I checked kept reporting on how it was apparently all under control. Probably to stop mass hysteria and panic. However it inevitably left people unprepared for what was surely about to happen.

Now this didn't happen in the space of a few days; the outbreak took months to reach us here in the UK. It got to the point we all believed we were safe.

The media had downplayed the impact of the virus just enough. The government had taken the proper precautions to ensure the safety of its people. Or so we thought. In fact, we were so confident in our country's ability to protect us that we decided to help other countries in need. Countless politicians gave grand speeches on how terrible the outbreak was, and how our hearts are with individuals, in these difficult times. There was even a broadcast from the Queen once the outbreak reached Paris.

We had a big concert and ploughed money into various charities which were set up almost overnight in order to help other countries in need. This did more damage than it did good.

We sent planes filled with food and medical supplies and countless volunteers and troops to help our European allies, only for them never to return again.

And what was I doing whilst this was all going on? Well, at first I carried on as normal. I went to work every day, I went home, spent time with my friends, my fiancé and my family. I carried on with life as normal, but I kept a close eye on the events unravelling before me.

I knew there was more to the virus than meets the eye. I tried to push my doubts to the back of my mind. I didn't want to believe that something bad was going to happen to us all. I felt sympathy towards the people who contracted the disease, but I couldn't empathise with them. I had no idea how it would feel being in that situation. I wasn't in it, and I hoped to God I never would be. That was enough for me.

I still checked the news on a daily basis; I monitored the events going on all over the world. All the facts pointed to a global outbreak of some sort. Although a zombie apocalypse seemed extremely far-fetched, I couldn't help but think that this is the closest thing to it I had ever heard. I have always had a tendency to be right, I didn't realise then how spot on I actually was.

The symptoms were worrying me. The way the virus transmitted was through blood, saliva and other bodily fluids. Now I'm not a medical expert, but if this is the only way it can be transmitted, then why is it affecting so many people so quickly? There had to be more to the story. Something they were leaving out in the news perhaps?

The symptoms were headaches, viral haemorrhagic fever, progressing to increased leakage of blood and fluids within the body, among many others. The virus took a week from infecting the host to death. My mind went straight to the film *28 DAYS LATER*. If any of you have seen the film, you will know the way the virus transmitted was identical. Perhaps Danny Boyle was onto something when he directed the film.

I waited, and I watched events unfold, and took in everything that was going on. Once it spread to the whole continent of Africa, I started to panic. I knew this couldn't be contained and that eventually it was going to make its way here, in England.

I watched news reports come in as the virus consumed Africa, then the Middle Eastern countries and eventually Europe.

Once the virus arrived in the UK, it caused complete chaos.

International flights had been cancelled long ago. Now all domestic flights ceased along with all train and bus operators. Public transport was no longer in existence. The only way to escape was by car or by foot.

Not that you could get anywhere fast. The amount of traffic blocked the roads were a nightmare; motorways were a complete no go.

When the virus finally spread to us, Dover was the first to be dramatically hit. It spread north, and London was compromised shortly after.

By this time, schools had been cancelled. Everyone had been advised to stay indoors and not to approach anyone who looked unwell or had a fever. Not everyone listened. Hospitals were the first to be infected, along with the built-up city areas.

At first the authorities were confident that the virus could be contained. When the authorities put all of their faith into the NHS, we knew we were all doomed. After another day or two it became apparent that there was no hope.

When it hit London, it was first compared to the Black Death with the trail of death and destruction it left in its path, but this was much worse.

We all saw on the TV what was going on. It was complete chaos. People flocked to nearby churches, mosques and synagogues praying to be spared, their last resort.

Bodies were littering the streets; those not infected were looting nearby shopping centres, grabbing anything and everything they could get their hands on. Fires were breaking out left, right and centre. Smoke could be seen in the distance coming from high-rise buildings, now ablaze. People were jumping out of buildings; trying to end it all before they got infected. Most preferred death to the infection. I wouldn't blame a single one of them. I've witnessed at first-hand what the virus can do, it was disturbing to see. People covered in pus-filled boils. Internal organs shutting down one by one, causing agonising pain to each and every victim it passes through.

The virus was spreading quickly. News reports were coming in thick and fast, from surrounding cities, towns and villages all over the southern regions. It was rapidly heading for the Midlands. It was only a matter of time before Birmingham collapsed. Once Birmingham went down, we knew that Manchester would be next.

Although we were getting news reports in daily, and we could see the catastrophe happening in front of our eyes, as far as we were concerned this was still, just a virus.

We were not aware at this point that the virus had mutated since it started its path of destruction, taking countless lives along its way. We certainly weren't aware the bodies were reanimating themselves and coming back from the dead. If I had known this, I wouldn't have left my bed, let alone my apartment.

At this time, the outbreak was currently raging in Birmingham. Yet all news reports and broadcasts assured us that the virus hadn't been seen this far up North.

I will always remember the day it first hit Manchester. I had my first encounter with an infected that day. It was also a personal milestone for me. It was the last time I would ever set foot in my office.

Chapter 2

Just Another Day at the Office

We were down to a skeleton staff. Since school had been cancelled, those with children had no choice but to stay at home. We were still waiting to hear back from those who lived in the outskirts of London and commuted on a weekly basis. We all saw the chaos on the news, yet we still held out hope that our colleagues were alive and safe.

That day, out of thirty office-based employees, only five of us had turned up. I had no choice but to go in that day. I was the only one who had keys to the office building and I needed to lock up.

The roads were extremely quiet that morning. In the eight miles it took me to get to work, I only saw three other cars on the road for my entire car journey. There wasn't a single soul on the road or pavement. There were no early morning runners or cyclists. I saw no pram-pushing mums. For a Monday, this was very unusual.

The atmosphere in the office was also a lot quieter than usual. Judging from the staff turnout, most people hadn't even bothered to show up. My fiancé Nick had decided to work from home that day. As I made my way through the side door and scanned my fob against the clocking-in machine, I secretly wished that I had done the same.

I sat myself down at my desk after swapping pleasantries with the colleagues who had bothered turning up. I switched my computer on and looked around me. Joyce had just come in and was hanging her coat up on the other side of the office.

Diane was sat at her desk, a few rows in front of me. She looked very pale; her eyes were reddening, and she was wiping them as if she had been crying. I would have gone over and comforted her, had she not been the heartless bitch we all knew. It sounds awful, but I didn't feel a shred of compassion for her, like everyone else in here, I hated her.

I had my reasons. She made everyone's life miserable; she took great pleasure in it. She was a vicious, over-opinionated evil bitch.

So why did I hate her? Well, once I had found my feet at the company, I was approached by the directors to undertake a highly confidential task. They wanted me to audit the phone lines, to make sure the calls were being handled correctly. I had a background in customer service and they thought that I would give them the most honest feedback, and remain impartial. I agreed and, as usual, got on with my own work. Once the results were in, her calls weren't looking so good. She was heard being rude and arrogant to customers, even putting the phone down on potential clients.

Now, I didn't know her very well at this point. We had spoken once or twice if that and I knew nothing about who she was, or what she did for the company.

Anyway, let's just say her telephone manner didn't go down very well with the directors at all. As far as I was concerned it wasn't my problem. I had done what I had been asked to do; it wasn't personal. I never pointed fingers or named names; I just wrote my report and included the recordings as evidence. At the end of the day, if we were losing business we needed to know about it.

When she found out I had written the report, rather than come to me about it, she decided to take her revenge. She started spreading a ridiculous rumour around that I was sleeping with one of the directors, she then had the audacity to say that the only reason I was getting ahead was because of my so-called affair. Let me get one thing straight. I didn't have to sleep with anyone to get ahead. I did that on merit alone.

I was completely outraged. I had recently got engaged and was perfectly happy in my own relationship. I couldn't even look at anyone else, let alone sleep with them. It took weeks for me to put an end to the rumours; my stress levels were rocketing. I even considered quitting. Of course, I told my fiancé Nick as soon as the rumours came to light. He was as angry as I, but he was extremely supportive of me, as always.

Anyway, Joyce had just made her way over to me and plonked herself on her desk, just next to mine.

"How are you coping, chicken?" she whispered to me. I could tell she was worried, she looked like she hadn't slept a wink.

"Surviving, as usual," I smiled weakly. "Are you okay?" I asked, now slightly concerned.

She looked to me and shook her head. "A few days ago Bobby went to Wolverhampton, to see his girlfriend. While all this was all going on in London! I told him not to go. He said he would be fine, but it's been two days and I haven't heard from him," she blurted out as she started to sob.

Bobby is her son; he's about the same age as me, quite tall but looks very young for his age. Joyce lived for her children; they were all she could talk about. She was so proud of them. She was a strong woman and kept her family close to her heart.

"Oh, Joyce, I'm sorry to hear that," I replied, giving her a big hug. "The phone lines have been a nightmare lately, you know this. I'm sure he's perfectly safe, he can look after himself. I bet he's more worried about you right now."

I tried to comfort her, but I knew my efforts could do no good. Nothing could ease her stress until her son was back home and safe.

Joyce looked up at me, "Yes, you're right. I'm just being daft. I'll be okay, don't you worry." She shook herself off, and as she did so, she looked over to Diane, who now looked as if she was burning up. "What's wrong with her?" she asked me, changing the subject. I could in tell, in the way she said HER with such disgust, that she shared the same opinion I did.

I shrugged my shoulders. "I have no idea. I haven't even spoken to her today. She doesn't look good though, does she?"

"I better go clean myself up and ask if she's okay," Joyce said, rolling her eyes. "Can I get you a brew, love?" she asked as she stood up.

I smiled and nodded as she picked my mug up and walked towards Diane.

I logged into my computer to check my email. I had no new emails. Usually my inbox had about fifty new emails every morning, I couldn't understand it, why didn't I have any? I clicked my send and receive button, just to make sure, but still nothing.

"Easy day for me then," I sighed.

Joyce wandered back over to me. "She doesn't look right at all, she's burning up! She says she's okay to work, but I don't know. I don't think she should be here," Joyce said.

"Wish she wasn't here, I thought she was crying earlier but then figured it can't be, she doesn't even have tear ducts!" I whispered bitchily, trying to cheer her up. Joyce smiled as she handed my mug back. "Have you been buying new shoes again?" she asked looking down at my feet, changing the subject completely.

"Uh... no?" I replied sheepishly. Out of the sixty-odd pairs of shoes I had, I could have sworn that woman memorised each pair. She had eyes like a hawk.

"You can't fool me. I don't know how that fiancé of yours keeps letting you buy them; you have more than enough." She carried on, "I keep telling you this, why won't you listen? You should put your money to better use my love. They are lovely though, I can't deny that."

Joyce never understood my love of shoes. She always said I had far too many, even when I complained I didn't have enough. I couldn't help myself. As Marilyn Monroe once said, 'Give a girl a pair of shoes, and she can conquer the world'. That's exactly how I feel in my favourite pair.

An hour or two passed. Neither of us said a word. Throughout the whole office, all you could hear was the clicking and clacking of various keyboards. In the silent office, the sound echoed all around us. The phone never rang.

All of a sudden we heard a gasp. Joyce and I looked up at the same time. Diane was sat still at her desk with blood pouring out from her nose. She was frantically trying to clear it up. She then grabbed her bag and pulled a handful of tissue out, put them on her nose, grabbed her keys and ran out the door.

"Told her she shouldn't have been here," remarked Joyce, bitterly.

"Now look at the mess she's left, inconsiderate cow," she tutted.

Now I don't know a great deal about why Joyce had such strong feelings towards Diane. But from what I had seen of her I couldn't blame her one bit.

Joyce never mentioned what had happened between them. Joyce wouldn't say boo to a goose, but once you get her in the same room as Diane, all hell breaks loose.

Another hour or so later, and Joyce and I were the only ones left in the building.

"Right, I think it's time we called it a day, don't you?" I turned to Joyce.

"Yes, I think you're right. There's not a lot we can do here anymore, and to be honest, love, I'd rather be at home. Just in case Bobby turns up," Joyce replied.

"Okay, sounds good to me. Would you mind making sure everything is okay here, and I will do a quick walkthrough of the factory and make sure the building's secure?" I asked. Joyce nodded.

I made my way down the stairs and onto the corridor leading to the factory floor. As soon as I turned the corner I looked down and saw the wad of bloody tissues Diane had run away with. That's disgusting, I thought to myself. Spots of blood trailed down the corridor and towards the factory.

"That's weird," I said to no one in particular. "Why would she head to towards the factory when the exit is the other way?"

I quickly dismissed it as I remembered that there was an industrial-sized paper dispenser in the entranceway of the factory.

"She obviously needed more," I thought to myself.

I made my way onto the factory floor. Even on a normal day it had an eerie feeling. It spanned across four units and without any of the machineries working it was as quiet as a mouse.

I made my way through the factory, glancing at each fire door as I walked past. This wasn't my favourite job at the best of times; I always hated walking around such a large old building on my own. It reminded me of the countless horror films I'd seen in which more often than not, the typical damsel in distress walks in unaware, and is met with her gruesome and untimely death.

I listened out for any sounds as I walked further into the units. The sound of my stilettos against the concrete floor echoed all around me.

I walked into the second unit. A few steps into this unit and I heard an ear-splitting clunk. I stopped dead in my tracks; I felt my heart drop to my stomach. The lights suddenly came on illuminating all the remaining units ahead of me.

I looked around me. Everything was silent and exactly how it should be. I suddenly realised the sound I heard was of the motion sensors in the building switching on the lights. I let out a sigh of relief and carried on with my checks. The feeling that I was not alone was evermore present.

I headed over to the shipping area; the gates were locked. The chain link fence that separates the shipping area from the factory was as it should be. It was still too quiet for my liking. I picked up my pace, eager to get out the office and on my way home.

I only had one unit to go. Then I was on the home stretch. As I walked through the printing area and into the packaging store, I felt my senses pick up.

I ignored it, keen to get back to Joyce and see the back end of this day. I looked all around checking off each door as I passed.

I started to hear a dripping noise coming from the far corner of the factory. It sounded as if water was coming through from above and hitting the steel railing on its way down. This was a completely normal sound, as our roof was always full of holes. On rainy days, it was common to see buckets scattered all around the factory floor catching various droplets that come through.

What wasn't normal, was the fact I heard this sound, yet it hadn't rained for months. I decided not to investigate. I wasn't about to spend more time than I needed to chasing after phantom droplets.

I carried on towards the entrance of the factory where I first originated from. The dripping noises seemed to be getting louder, the closer I got to the entrance.

I got halfway towards the entrance when I looked up. There, on the staircase leading up to the office, was Diane, hunched over a man lying half way up the stairs. On closer inspection I realised it was John the caretaker.

Something about the whole situation didn't seem right. I was about to run up to them to find out what had happened, when something inside me stopped me. I realised the sound of dripping water was in fact coming from them. More specifically, it was coming from John. I followed the droplets down with my eyes and noticed a dark puddle forming just underneath where they lay.

It didn't take me long to figure out what was happening. He hadn't moved at all since I saw them; the puddle was most definitely blood. My eyes shifted back to Diane. She hadn't noticed me as she was far too engrossed in her meal.

I stood there, not daring to move. I could hear the sound of muscle being bitten into; it was as if she was biting into a fresh juicy peach. That thought alone put me off peach for life. More blood poured out from her mouth and down his arm, the sound of bone grinding against her teeth were like nails on a chalkboard. As she bit down even further I could hear the crunching and snapping of his smaller and more brittle bones.

I felt sick, not daring to move in case I made my presence known. She hadn't even glanced in my direction, so I knew I was okay for now, as long as she didn't notice me.

I needed to get out. However, I knew that every step I took could be heard. I looked down and quickly decided that the shoes needed to go.

I slowly slid off my black stilettos, balancing on each foot whilst I slid the other foot out, trying my hardest not to make a single sound.

It was clear that the only way I would be able to get past her would be to sneak around the factory unnoticed and slip out the front door.

Luckily the staircase she was currently grazing on was used as an emergency exit only. No one had ever used that as an entrance to the office, and I knew it could only be opened from inside of the office. It meant Joyce was safe, for now at least.

I needed to focus. All I needed to do was slip out the factory and into the office, grab my keys and get myself home.

I picked up my abandoned heels and started to tiptoe slowly towards the other side of the factory. I never took my eyes off Diane. She carried on eating her meal, paying me no attention whatsoever.

I turned my gaze to the floor. I was completely barefoot and the last thing I needed was a loose nail jabbing me in the foot.

I manoeuvred around the machinery, crouching down so I couldn't be seen. Every so often I'd stop, just to check she was still there.

Before long I was near the factory entrance and on the home straight. I looked up again to make sure Diane was still preoccupied with the remains of our once lovable caretaker.

She was still next to John, yet her focus was now on me. I froze. She tilted her head and looked at me curiously, as if weighing me up.

I didn't give her a chance to figure out what her options were. Jumping over the last few pieces of machinery, I ran through the corridor and upstairs to Joyce.

"We need to go –*now*," I warned, still breathless from my recent ordeal.

"What's going on, love, you look a bit peachy?" Joyce asked, surprised.

"I don't have time to explain, and I don't really know what's happening, it's not safe, Joyce. We need to go!" I was pretty much pulling her out of the door at this point.

Before she had time to protest, we heard a dull thud against the glass in the office. It was coming from the staircase where Diane had been previously.

Diane was stood at the window which overlooks the factory, smearing her blood-soaked hands over the glass. Her expression was one I had never seen, one of pure anger and frustration. Hunger. She looked like she was trying to bite her way through the door. When she realised this wasn't working, she started banging her head against the glass instead.

We stood watching her for a few seconds until cracks started to appear within the glass.

"Let's go!" I pulled at Joyce one last time and we both ran out the building and towards our cars as fast as our legs could carry us.

As soon as we got to our cars, she looked at me. "I don't know what's going on, but whatever it is, it's here. I want you to get in your car now and drive home. Don't stop for anyone just get there. I'll do the same."

I wasn't going to argue with her; I've never seen her speak so forcefully.

Her toned softened. "I don't want anything to happen to you chicken, just promise me you'll stay safe and do as I say. Text me when you get home, so I know your safe."

I nodded and promised her I would do as she said. With that we both got into our cars and went our separate ways.

As I drove home, the scene before me was unreal. I thought I was in hell. As I was driving through villages, people around me were running into the road, breaking into shops and screaming and shouting. They were pleading for their lives.

I did as Joyce said. I didn't stop for anyone at all. I had to swerve countless times to avoid pedestrians running out in front of my car.

Once or twice I had to stop the car completely as people banged on the bonnet of my car screaming to be let in. My white car was covered in bloody handprints.

I threw my car into reverse and drove around them. It was complete madness outside; I knew I couldn't trust anyone. I just needed to get home.

Chapter 3

Holding Up

After an eventful journey and multiple detours and roadblocks, I finally pulled up in the car park to our apartment block. I decided to park in the space nearest to the apartments. I figured it would come in useful for a quick getaway if necessary. It wasn't my official allocated space, but I didn't care. I'm sure the couple whose space this was, were already long gone.

I looked all around me; my heart was still beating out my chest. The whole complex seemed quiet. Luckily most of the people who lived here were all professionals of some sort. Most would still be at work; those who weren't must have already left to find family members, or anyone who was significantly important to them.

I didn't stick around long enough to find out; I sat there a few seconds, too terrified to move. I took a deep breath and threw my door open. I tried to launch myself out the car and towards the entrance door, which was only a few yards away.

I pushed off from my steering wheel, about to make a run for it, only to be violently pulled back into my seat.

Perfect. I was trapped. My heart stopped. I thought that was going to be the end for me. I couldn't even let out a scream. The fear was paralysing.

I sat waiting to feel cold hands tearing at my clothes, gripping onto me before hungrily biting down on my shoulders and neck. Succumbing me to the virus that had already taken millions.

I waited a couple of seconds, but nothing happened. "What the hell is going on?" I asked myself.

I looked down, and I realised. I hadn't taken my seatbelt off. A gush of relief ran through me. I couldn't help but laugh to myself. I quickly undid the belt and grabbed my keys. My mind was starting to think rationally again. I found the door key and made my way, swiftly into the entrance.

My apartment was the first door at the top of the staircase. I couldn't hear a thing from any of the other homes, so I started to make my way up the stairs. All of a sudden, I started to hear rustling coming from the corridor below. On any other day I would have completely ignored it. It was normal; people come in and out all the time. But, right now nothing was normal. I picked up my pace and let myself in.

As soon as I got through the door, I turned and immediately slammed it shut as fast as my hands could manage. For the first time since living there, I used the second deadlock on the door. I was safe for now.

I looked around the flat. Everything was how I left it. I looked up, and there in the doorway was my fiancé, Nick. He looked at me and smiled. That cheesy grin I first fell in love with. Of course, he had seen from the window my whole seatbelt fiasco. He had seen my struggle and my pathetic dash for safety.

I could feel my cheeks blushing. "Do not say a word!" I warned him, grinning.

"I wouldn't dream of it, baby," he responded coolly. "I'm just glad you're home safe."

I looked up at him and smiled. Even in my highest heels he still towered over me. At six foot two, he towered over most people. His broad shoulders accentuated his slim yet muscly physique. His dark hair perfectly contrasted against his bright blue eyes. Just looking at him made my knees go week, even after the three years we had been together.

I practically fell into his arms; he pulled me close and kissed my forehead. For a few seconds I forgot about what was going on around us, I was just relieved he was okay, and that he was here with me.

I walked through into our living room and looked around. Sat there on the sofa I saw Lola and her husband, Andy. They looked slightly shaken up, but Lola's face was masked by the same false Cheshire cat smile that I had seen many times before.

Now although Lola has been a friend for some time, well more of an acquaintance, she wasn't my favourite person in the world. In fact, she never even made the list.

From the outside she was a pretty girl, she came across very conservative but had a nice slim, slender figure. She had very light blonde hair, and very pale skin. She was a typical dainty English rose type.

For as pleasant as she looked from the outside, on the inside I always said she made Quasimodo look like a beauty queen. She had no common sense whatsoever. She also managed, in the past, to piss off a lot of my close friends with her shameful, yet cringe worthy behaviour.

She was very two faced. She turned up her nose at everyone and had a holier than thou attitude. I've often thought in a past life she must have been one of those strict Catholic nuns, the ones you used to see often in old-fashioned schools.

She had to have an opinion on everything, but made out she had a perfect life. The reality was far from. She was extremely possessive of her husband Andy; she had him completely whipped. I have to admit we all felt sorry for the poor guy. He was the only reason we tolerated her.

She spent most of her time pouting in front of the mirror, looking at herself in different angles, there was no one she could possibly love more than she did herself. We called her Duckface when she wasn't around, although, truth be told she looked more of a cross between a duck and a chipmunk with the false smile she always gave off. What I would do to wipe that smile off her face, it wound me up no end.

Her husband Andy, on the other hand, was very down to earth. He had a calm and gentle manner, nothing seemed to faze him. Like I said, we all felt sorry for him. His wife was extremely high maintenance and very controlling. You could tell she wore the trousers in the relationship. I wish he had the courage to grow some balls and put her in her place. You could tell he wasn't happy. We all figured he just stayed with her to keep the peace. Although, collectively, we thought he would be much better off on his own.

As a couple they didn't look right together. Andy was very fit and active. He loved all outdoor sports, especially rock climbing and sea fishing. Andy and Nick often went on fishing and camping trips together; it's how they became so close.

Andy wasn't as broad as Nick was. He was slightly shorter than average, at five foot eleven. Like Nick, he had dark hair but was always clean shaven.

I wasn't exactly pleased to see them, but there was nothing I could do about it now. As much as I wanted to throw Duckface out and see her savaged by the virus that was infecting everyone else, I just wasn't that heartless. I certainly didn't want to see Andy have to face it alone out there; we were all much safer inside.

"What are you guys doing here?" I asked, secretly hoping they had just come round for a quick brew before going back to their own house. They did nothing but brag about it, so why couldn't they just stay there?

"I saw what was happening in the news, and I had just had to come and make sure you guys were okay," said Lola in her all too familiar patronising tone.

I wasn't born yesterday. I know full well that she doesn't give a crap about anyone else, unless it was for her own personal gain, of course. My guess is that she knew she was a sitting duck (literally) in her specially made glass-fronted house and knew that there was safety in numbers so she decided to come to us for safety.

"How nice of you, but yes we're fine now," came my equally sarcy reply. I dug my nails into Nick's hand, a silent reminder that I was not overly impressed.

Ignoring my less than friendly response, she carried on. "Well, now we're all together – and safe, thank God! – I think we should all stick together. Besides when it comes down to it, I don't think I feel completely safe on my own."

There it is! The real reason she came. She was too scared to deal with this herself, so she came running to us for help. It didn't go unnoticed that she had not acknowledged Andy in any of this. But that didn't matter to her. As with everything in life, it was all about her.

"Great, so I guess we're stuck with them now." I hissed to Nick when we were finally alone in the kitchen. He just shrugged. "Yeah, it's not ideal but not a fat lot we can do about it now. Never should have let them in."

I just nodded. I knew he shared the same opinion as me when it came to Duckface. She really was that irritating. But he was right. Not a fat lot we can do about it, but make the most of a bad situation.

I suddenly remembered I hadn't texted Joyce. I grabbed my phone from my bag and quickly typed her message:

Hi, made it home safe! Nicks here as well as some irritating house guests. U ok? Xx

I quickly sent the message; I kept checking my phone eagerly awaiting a reply. To this day I never received a response.

Getting back to the matter at hand, we needed a way to keep the infected out and ourselves in. I told Nick, Andy and Duckface what happened on the factory floor and recounted my journey home.

We decided the first thing we needed to do was to construct a barricade for the door. If one thing was for sure, it wasn't just the infected we needed to defend ourselves from, it was the panicked looters and rioters that could prove to be an issue as well.

Luckily our flat had a little entrance cove, similar to a porch. This had another door to the right, which opened to the main hallway of the flat. We decided to grab what we could and fill the entrance completely from top to bottom, so that in case the door locks were compromised, there was no way that anyone or anything was getting inside.

We started scouring the flat trying to find anything we didn't need to block off the entranceway. We dismantled wardrobes, tables and chairs and propped them up alongside the ironing board, a sofa and anything else we could get our hands on. Given the current events, which were in the forefront of all our minds, I figured ironing would end up being a thing of the past.

Once the barricade was up and we were confident nothing was getting in uninvited, my mind drifted to the other issues at hand.

We didn't know how long this pandemic was going to last. I had seen on the news how quickly it spread, but knew very little about the virus itself. I had one encounter with the infected, and I wasn't in a rush to repeat that.

A couple of hours later, I was exhausted. The day's events had completely drained me. I felt safe enough in the apartment; I just wanted to go to bed. I was sick of making small talk with Duckface, and had stopped listening to her hours ago. Nick and I purposely left the guest room bed intact when barricading the door, so we offered this to them.

We took ourselves off to bed and settled down for the night, not knowing what we were in for the next day.

"What are we going to do?" I asked Nick once we were alone. "We can't stay in here forever."

He pulled me in close. "I don't know, baby, I don't know of anywhere we can go just yet. Don't worry about it, you're safe now – just try and go to sleep."

I turned into him and buried my head into his shoulder as he wrapped his arms around me tighter, and eventually I drifted off.

I woke up at eight the next morning. It was a rough night; the apartment was boiling, so we were forced to open the windows. The air outside felt thick and heavy. It smelt like bonfire night; it was as if a raging fire was burning just a couple miles away. There probably was. Screams and cries for help could be heard in all directions, making sleep a near impossible task.

I'm not too sure what time I finally drifted off; Nick held me tightly all night. If he hadn't, I don't think I would have slept at all. Even before any of this happened the safest place for me was in his arms. I would always say to him, "I don't care where we are or what we're doing, as long we're together, I'm happy."

I know, you're probably all reaching for your sick buckets right about now, but it's true. Even more so now. It is the only place I truly felt at ease.

Nick was still asleep, and I couldn't hear the other two stirring. I decided to take a look out the bedroom window and see for myself what destruction, if any, last night's events had left.

As a safety precaution, we closed all curtains and blinds throughout the apartment when we were barricading the door. We didn't want to alert anyone to our presence, either dead or alive. We knew there would be other survivors out there, but the risk was too great. We needed to look after ourselves. We only had limited supplies, and we needed them to last as long as possible. Any other mouths to feed would just be a burden. We didn't have anything to offer them.

As I got closer to the curtains, I froze on the spot, trying to listen out for any movement both inside and out. When I was confident no sound could be heard, I leaned against the wall. Pulling the curtain back a few inches, I peered out the side of the window, making sure I couldn't be seen from the outside.

The sight before me was surreal. Shopping trolleys littered the pavement. Rubbish was strewn everywhere, floating in the wind. Pools of blood dotted the roads and gardens.

However, more disturbingly, the owners of said blood were nowhere to be seen.

It looked as if we were living on one of the roughest council estates of Wythenshawe. Not a high-end apartment building on the outskirts of Wilmslow.

I looked into the distance, past the abandoned shopping trolleys and path of destruction.

There, stood on the corner, staring into the road, was a young girl. She was dressed in her pyjamas and holding what looked like a fluffy toy rabbit. She was swaying from side to side as if with the wind. She seemed completely mesmerised by the empty road she was fixating on.

The more I stared at her, the more I came to recognise her. She lived on one of the new-build houses to the left of our apartment. I had never spoken to her but had often seen her in the summer playing with her friends and her other siblings.

She was a plump short girl, and I had no doubts in my mind that the poor girl had Down's syndrome. She stood out to me, as she would always be running a few paces behind the others. Once or twice I'd seen and heard arguments break out between her friends, if and when one of them had said something horrible to her. They were irritating and loud at times. But they seemed a good bunch of kids.

I couldn't take my eyes off her; she didn't look injured, but at the same time something was not right about her at all. She was usually a smiley, happy child with rosy cheeks. Now, she looked very pale and had an eerie, vacant expression as she stared at, well, nothing. I knew she had not seen me and she was not facing in my direction.

All of a sudden she dropped what she was holding, she turned and walked off slowly into the distance. As she wandered away, I noticed her right foot was bent out of place. It looked like a bone was protruding through her ankle. This didn't seem to faze her at all; it just seemed to slow her down slightly, as she shuffled with each step.

My eyes drew back to the fluffy toy rabbit she had discarded. Only it wasn't a toy rabbit, judging from the blood and bones sticking out at all angles – it was without a doubt real. And dead.

The blood on the rabbit's fur had darkened, and the bones were a bright white. They had been licked completely clean. It was obviously once a sweet childhood pet. She must have found it in one of the gardens, if not her own.

I turned away from the window, feeling slightly sick. I didn't tell anyone else about the girl I had seen. I didn't want anyone to panic – we needed to figure out a plan and keep ourselves alive, that was the main concern.

As soon as everyone was awake, I gathered them in the living room. We discussed our options until it became clear that none of us were in a rush to leave the apartment in the immediate future.

This being said we still needed a plan. Nothing was certain anymore. The undead weren't our only problem. Right now we had internet, we had TV and we had electricity, gas and water. For how long, none of us knew.

As a first point of call, we left Duckface and Andy to check the food supplies. We had collectively decided that it was best to use up the fresh food first as this had the shortest shelf life. We would then move onto the frozen food, just in case we lost power, and the freezer defrosted itself.

Whilst they got to work on making an inventory of the entire food contents, we started filling up bottles, containers, glasses, anything we could find with water. Just in case our water supply got shut off, or worse, contaminated. We even filled the sinks and bath just so we had as much water as possible.

We then went on the hunt for medical supplies. We had an abundance of hay fever tablets, a couple of boxes of paracetamol, imodium and travel sickness tablets. We had half a box of Disney Princess plasters and a digital thermometer. We had no antibiotics and no substantial first aid kit. All in all, we were not doing well on the medical front.

"Babe, you still have those ridiculous Princess plasters?" Nick asked me when he found them.

"Yep, why wouldn't I? They're pink and pretty and have princesses on them!" I replied.

"Okay, whatever makes you happy." He rolled his eyes. "Bloody Princess plasters," he muttered.

"What was that?" I asked.

"Love you," he replied, mockingly.

"Thought so!" I shouted to him, ignoring his sarcasm as I crossed the room.

Once we had all the information together, we figured we had about three weeks' worth of food and water, as long as we rationed well. Our medical supplies needed work, but there was nothing we could do about that now.

"So what do we do when we've got no more food left?" Duckface asked.

"I have no idea," I shrugged.

"We'll figure it out when it comes to it. None of us really know what's going on out there. Who knows? It might die down in a few days," said Andy, optimistic as ever.

"That might be the case, but I suggest we prepare for the worst. Just to be on the safe side" Nick said, thinking more realistically.

We needed to know as much as possible about what we were facing. So we switched on the TV, and were speechless as we took in the carnage unravelling before our eyes. Firefighters were running around trying desperately to put out burning buildings, whilst people ran screaming in every direction. Groups of the infected could be seen hunting in packs, chowing down on innocent passers-by. Abandoned police cars and ambulances were left in the road. Some had been left after crashing into other cars and telephone poles. It was complete bedlam.

"This video footage was taken last night in the city centre of Manchester. The emergency services have been unable to contain the outbreak. The current death toll for Manchester has now reached over a hundred thousand in the last forty-eight hours," came the voice from the newscaster.

"The government has urged all citizens to stay indoors. Do not open the door for anyone – I repeat, do not open the door for anyone."

The screen jumped back to the scenes we had just witnessed. It was a repeat broadcast.

We sat there for a few minutes in complete and utter silence. All the hairs on my arm stood up, and I couldn't help but shiver.

"Is this really happening?" I finally broke the silence.

"I believe so" Andy solemnly replied. "I suggest we do as they say. We're safe here; we're certainly not going to let anyone else in, and there's not a chance I'm going out there" his previous optimism fading fast.

"We need to find out more about this virus, I don't know what's caused this, but I am not going to end up like those things walking around out there," Nick added.

From out of nowhere, Duckface shrieked, "Oh my God! No, I can't believe it – Jane's dead!"

I felt an eye roll coming on as the sound of her annoying voice began to grate on me.

We all turned to her. "How the hell do you know that?" I asked as I tried to compose myself.

She looked up from her phone. "It's on Facebook!" she exclaimed. "Sophie has just posted this, look."

The post read like this:

Idk what's going on here, but I've just been attacked by some weirdo on my way home, I'm fine but Jane got hurt. He bit her in the neck, and she fell. There was blood everywhere and she didn't make it. Someone please help Wtf do I do?!

I scrolled down, and her newsfeed was filled with posts asking for help, and RIP messages for the fallen and infected friends and family members. There were even a few sick videos – killings up close.

I handed back her phone. I couldn't believe what was going on, and how far this had spread in such a short amount of time.

My mind went back to the factory floor. The sight of the poor old caretaker John being devoured by my ex-colleague Diane. It was horrific, and it was going on all around us. I thought back to the way Diane looked at the window in the office. She had no emotion, just a vacant, blank expression as she tried to smash her way through the glass, yet beneath her diabolical exterior, I felt something more sinister. I just couldn't place what it was.

The sound of a camera shutter brought me back from my daydream. I looked towards the sound. Despite all the chaos and misery going on all around us, Duckface was sat on the end of our sofa, holding the phone up whilst tilting her head, her lips puckered. I couldn't believe it; she was taking a selfie!

I couldn't bite my tongue any more. "What the hell are you doing, you vain, inconsiderate bitch!" I screamed at her. "People are dying all around us, and all you can do is take pictures of yourself. You don't give a shit about anyone else. That's it, either get your head of your arse or get the fuck out of my house." I couldn't bite my tongue any longer. She never went out of her way for anybody. Why should I show her any courtesy?

She said nothing. She just glared at me, without saying a word she got up and stormed into the guest room. She acted like a stroppy teenager.

I wasn't sorry. She was in dire need of a reality check. No one got up to follow her out, even Andy stayed with us. He looked towards me apologetically.

"Right, we need to figure out what we're going to do. We can't stay here forever, eventually we're going to run out of food. I'm already starting to go stir crazy trapped in here."

Nick and Andy nodded. We tossed ideas back and forth. "As long as we have electricity, I think we need to make the most of it. We don't know how long it's going to last."

I agreed with Nick. We grabbed every single electronic device we could get our hands on. Phones, laptops, tablets, everything that could be charged got plugged in. We decided to keep all devices charging at all times, just in case.

I spent the rest of that day cooking all the fresh and frozen food, freezing what I could, just in case we lost power. 'Just in case' was becoming the phrase of the day.

We spent the next three days after that making our way through our entire film collection, just to keep ourselves occupied. In this time Duckface and I never spoke a word to each other. Quite frankly, I preferred it that way. I couldn't stand her at the best of times. Tolerating her was becoming an impossible task.

The screams from the outside world that could be heard were less and less constant. Nights became more peaceful as the noise died down. Still we kept the curtains closed. No one ever looked out, as far as we were all concerned we did not want to see, hear or smell the outside world. We stayed quiet and kept to ourselves, we only found out what was happening through the news, which was now broadcast on every channel.

On the fourth day, we finally lost power and water. It wasn't a great surprise; we already had T-light candles placed in various rooms of the apartment. We were as prepared as we could be, given the circumstances.

We unplugged all our phones and switched them off. No point in wasting the battery until we absolutely had to.

Things were starting to get difficult for us all. We no longer knew what was happening in the outside world. There was no sign of rescue. We spent our days waiting, for what? We didn't quite know.

Duckface finally broke the silence between us. "There's something I need to show you," she whispered, "I've been checking up on Facebook to find out what's going on. People have been posting different theories about what's happening. Don't be mad, but I made a group."

"What do you mean you've made a group – what for?" I asked.

"Well, our family and friends are out there. I made the group so we could all keep in contact with each other. Don't worry I haven't told anyone we're here." She carried on. "There might be a safe place somewhere, somewhere we can go nearby."

This was the first time I had ever heard her talk like that. Making a Facebook group seemed like an odd thing to do, but at least she was trying to help. I didn't think she had it in her. My feelings towards her began to mellow.

"Why are you telling me this now?" I asked.

"When the electricity went off I knew I couldn't carry it on, not on my own. I know we need to save our battery power just in case. But there's still people online."

She handed me her phone. I opened the page. She had named it 'E Virus Support Group'.

I couldn't help but laugh. It sounded like some form of AA meeting for alcoholics, drug users and people with other strange addictions.

I looked down the page. She already had two thousand members. This was good, it meant other people were alive and well.

People were posting all sorts of messages to the group. Most posts were cries for help. A few were sharing their experiences; a few had mentioned being bitten or injured.

I had to hand it to her; it was a good idea. We needed to keep track of what was going on in some way. This seemed like our only option. I decided to give her a chance.

We decided to monitor the online group once a day. That way we weren't constantly checking it and could reserve power. It was now our only link with the outside world.

We lost our Wi-Fi connection when we lost power. We were now solely relying on the 3G from our phones. Without any of us venturing outside, we already felt we were living in the most primal of ways. We had no idea what were in for.

Chapter 4

The Search for Supplies

As time went on our food supplies were starting to deplete rapidly. After two weeks stuck in the apartment, we were down to only canned goods. I missed my old life, where online food shopping was at the click of a button.

Even the water was drying out, and although we had hung a bucket from the kitchen window to harvest rainwater, the weather conditions were proving difficult. It hadn't rained for days.

We spent our days completely closed off from the outside world. We still hadn't opened the curtains or checked outside.

We were doing what we could to keep ourselves occupied. We read books, played games and told stories. Some days, none of us even bothered getting out of bed.

We were struggling for things to do, we had very few books in the apartment, without the luxury of TV, Internet even radio, we were cut off from what we relied on most.

Tempers were rising between all of us; traits that we wouldn't usually notice were becoming extremely irritating. The apartment felt like it was shrinking, with each passing hour.

Duckface was starting to get on my nerves. The sound of her voice began to grate on me even further. Every time she spoke I could feel the anger welling up inside of me, I found it harder and harder to keep the peace.

Nick and I were starting to get irritated with each other. It's not healthy in any relationship to spend twenty-four hours a day with each other. I was even starting to miss work, just for the peace and quiet and change of scenery.

Each day felt the same; it was like Groundhog Day. It was the same routine day in and day out.

We were running low on candles. Each night we sat in the pitch black, with not even the faintest of streetlights to provide us with any light. Now, even in the dark we didn't have to feel our way around the apartment. We had been there that long we knew where each door, wall and piece of furniture was. We could walk around effortlessly, dodging each obstruction as if we could see clear as day. We were far too familiar with our surroundings.

We needed to get out. We had spent far too much time in the same company. Claustrophobia, impatience and depression were starting to reveal themselves, and were becoming frequent emotions in our everyday lives.

"We need to start thinking about getting out of here. Our food isn't going to last very long, and I think you'll all agree it's not healthy, cooped up in here." I took charge of the situation.

"But where are we going to go? And what are we going to do?" Duckface asked.

"I don't know. But we need to think of something guys. What do you all think? I'm open to suggestions," I said slightly irritated.

Andy chimed in. "Okay, before we go out all guns blazing, let's have a serious think about this. We don't know what's out there; we don't know how many there are and more importantly we don't know where they are."

He was right. We didn't know what we were in for, beyond that door was a mystery to us all.

"Why don't we search the building for supplies? Food? Water? Anything we can use?" Nick added.

It was a good idea. But it had a major flaw. Just how exactly were we going to get into the other apartments? We could smash our way through the doors, but we didn't want to attract any attention. Plus we didn't know what would be waiting for us on the other side.

"And how exactly are we going to get in, babe?" I asked.

"I don't know. We need to find something to wedge open the door, without making any noise," he replied.

"Wait, I have a crowbar!" Andy exclaimed. "One problem though, it's in the boot of my car."

Great, to get anywhere inside, we first had to go outside.

I stood up and made my way to the bay window. "Right I've had enough, I think it's time we took a look outside."

They all agreed. We all stood at each side of the window. Duckface and Andy on one side, Me and Nick on the other. We didn't want anyone or anything to know we were here.

Duckface and I crouched down; we crawled under the curtain and peered over the windowsill.

The sight before us was similar to my last glimpse of the new world. Everything was how I remembered. Trolleys were still left abandoned, and rubbish was still building up covering parts of the pavements and roads.

All in all, it was very quiet. Not a soul could be seen dead or alive. We could see Andy's car from the window. It was six spaces down from us, about twenty meters away. It wasn't far at all. It looked safe enough. The complex was very open plan; we could see everything from where we were. We were on the second floor out of three.

We decided to ditch the covert operation and pull the curtains back to get a better view. We all peered out the window.

Now where we lived, there were three individual apartment blocks. Each split into two, with six apartments in each segment. Within each segment there were two exits, one at the front and another at the back.

Within in the whole complex there were around thirty-six apartments. All the buildings together formed an upside-down U shape. They all faced towards a small open garden, in which a small oak tree grew in the centre. The lawn was always perfectly manicured, and all hedges and flower beds were always neat and tidy.

All in all it wasn't a big complex; it was in a nice quiet neighbourhood, just off the A34. However, it was set far enough away that traffic noise did not reach us, it was in a perfect location.

The cars were parked just off the road; each space faced in towards the garden. We looked into the road, on the pavements surrounding the apartments, and still no one could be seen.

"Okay, what about this? Two of us make our way outside, whilst the other two take watch. Go over to the car, get the crowbar and come back. On the way back check as many windows as we can to see if there's anyone inside?" I suggested.

They all looked at me and looked back at one another. They all agreed to it. It seemed pretty straightforward plan, as far as plans go.

Nick and Andy decided it was best if they go. Duckface and I stayed behind. We all started removing the makeshift barricade we had created on our first night. Once there was a clear path to the door, we all got into position.

Duckface and I had agreed between ourselves that one of us would keep watch; the other would stay near the door to let the boys back in, and scout for any unwanted visitors.

The boys had decided to first find some makeshift weapons, just in case they got into any trouble. Nick found a yellow and black hammer next to his toolbox, whilst Andy decided to wait until he got his crowbar, and use that if needed.

It became evident we needed to find some more efficient weapons once we gained access to the other apartments. I wished as a country we were more like the Americans. Guns would have come in so useful at this point.

I had used guns before. In fact, my aim was perfect; I could hit the same spot twice. Dad taught me how to shoot growing up. He had a big air rifle, a real heavy old-fashioned thing. He used to take me to the derelict outbuildings we had. He would point at a pane of glass, and I'd shoot it. After I'd shot the glass, he would get me to target the exact same spot I had just hit. I got it dead on more often than not. After my first few goes, it was apparent that my shot was far more accurate than his ever could be. He didn't like that very much, but we both enjoyed it, and it brought us closer together. I had never hit a moving target, but how hard could it be?

I decided it was best to let Duckface keep watch from the window. I didn't trust her at the door. It was better for her to stand at the window; I was worried that at the first sign of trouble she would panic and lock the door, and then Nick and Andy would be trapped outside. It wouldn't surprise me in the slightest. She was never the most trustworthy of people.

Before the boys left we all took turns checking the peephole and listening for movement. So far so good, nothing could be seen or heard. Carefully opening the door and making sure we didn't make any noise, the boys headed out. I held the door open and kept it open as I watched them walk downstairs and out the entrance.

Everything seemed normal so far. The corridor and staircase looked exactly the same as it did the last time I was out there. So far, everything was intact. It was going well. I made my way back inside, towards the bedroom window, to get a better view on where they were. I hated the idea of Nick being out there, if something was to happen to him, I don't know what I would do. It was as if a part of me was out there as well.

Once the boys were outside I could see them looking around, checking the coast was clear. I was as they slowly made their way to the car; Nick always kept three paces behind Andy; he never let his guard down. They got to the car and swiftly into the boot. Whilst Andy rummaged around trying to find the crowbar, Nick stood in front checking over his shoulders, making sure they weren't attracting any unwanted attention. It was like watching a covert military operation. I was proud of us all.

As soon as Andy had a handle on the crowbar they made their way to the ground floor windows. We decided that they should take a look around the flats in our own building, staying as close to home as possible. I had hoped we would be able to secure at least our block, so we had a bit more freedom, and could stay a bit longer. Maybe Duckface and Andy could claim one of the apartments as their own, giving me and Nick some much needed time to ourselves.

As they passed each window they gave us a nod, so we knew they were clear. We lost sight of them as they moved around the back. I darted to the next bedroom to get a clearer view. I didn't want to let either of them out of my sight.

I checked all around the back. From the window, I could see all the way to the end of the buildings. I waited for the boys to reappear; whilst I was waiting, I checked the area to make sure they were definitely alone.

As I glanced towards the opposite end of the building and into the rear car park, I could see movement coming from behind a car. It looked too big to be an animal, from the shadows it looked as it was almost hunched over.

As the boys reappeared, they were clearly feeling more confident. They carried on checking each window, taking longer to peer in than they had previously.

As the boys were absorbed in checking the contents of the apartments the huddled figure rose, disturbed by the noise the boys were making. It was the old man from downstairs. I recognised him instantly. His eyes were red, and a big red bloodstain was covering his once pale blue shirt.

He was infected; there was no doubt about it. Blood covered his mouth. He almost didn't look real. He was as pale as a china doll; his skin had the texture of a wax figure. His face was expressionless. He followed the boys with his eyes but made no attempt to move.

I knew I had to warn them. They clearly hadn't noticed him standing there. They were gradually making their way closer and closer to the infected man. I wanted to bang on the windows to grab their attention, but I knew any further noise would alert the man. Duckface had seen what I had. Slowly, she opened the window. The sound of the window opening diverted the boys' attention. I ran into the kitchen where Duckface was standing and put my finger in front of my mouth. "Don't say a word," I whispered as I pushed her out the way.

I moved towards the window. I mouthed for the boys to turn around. As they turned the infected man began to shuffle his way towards them. I saw the look of horror as they took one look at him and ran. I'm sure one of them let out a shriek of some sort. I quickly made my way back to the door to let them back in. They came flying up the stairs and launched themselves into the apartment and fell into a heap on the floor in the entranceway.

"So much for being big and brave," I teased.

"Shut up," they both mumbled, helping each other off the floor.

The first part of our plan was a success. We partly barricaded the door back up, and all went and sat in the living room to discuss Phase 2.

As the boys were outside they only managed to check the two ground floor apartments nearest to us, we had no idea what was on the other side of the doors in the third floor apartments or next door.

We decided that we would start on with the ground floor. We knew it was relatively safe, and the boys were certain no one was in there.

I decided to go with them this time. I was confident I could do it; I was starting to understand the way the infected acted. Although I hadn't been in close contact with any of them, I had seen more than the rest had. I'd also seen more zombie films than anyone here put together. I thought I had a good idea of what I was in for.

"I'm coming with you," I told Nick matter-of-factly.

"No, you're fucking not," Nick protested.

"I am, I know what we need and I can look after myself. Lola's fine here on her own anyway, aren't you?" I asked pointing at her.

"Actually... I," I cut her off before she could get another word out "See, its fine. I'm coming, there's nothing you can say to stop me," I told him firmly.

"Okay, fine. But stay close to me, I don't want you out my sight."

I rolled my eyes, "Babe, we're going downstairs, not across the country."

With that, I went to scour the flat for a suitable weapon. I needed something light but effective. I'm not very strong, so to carry something heavy would do more damage than it would good. My strength was my speed, so I needed to take advantage of that. I debated using a kitchen knife, but I would need strength to be able to cause any real damage, strength that I just didn't have. Lucky for me, a knife was Andy's weapon of choice. I eventually decided to borrow his crowbar.

Then, like all girls would in this situation. I went to find an appropriate outfit. I decided to go for my leather knee-high boots; they had a small chunky heel and were one of my comfiest pairs to walk in. The leather was thick, so I figured that at least from the knee down I was unbitable. I teamed the boots with my black skinny jeans and a long-sleeved tight top. I didn't want any of my clothes getting caught on anything, and I felt safer knowing all my skin was covered.

Once I was happy with my ensemble, we made our way to the first apartment. We all felt it was best to leave Duckface upstairs. She was more than happy to do so. After I gave her a lecture of what she can and can't do I felt okay leaving her there. It was like having to negotiate with a child. I took my keys just in case; I still didn't trust her.

The corridor below us was pitch black. The power was out, so none of the lights worked. The only light we had was coming through the glass window on the entrance door.

Nick opened the corridor door leading to the ground floor apartments, and we all stood back. It was quiet; Nick and Andy wandered through, and I stayed at the door, letting the limited light we had fill the corridor in front of us.

They stopped outside apartment 32. This was the infected man's apartment. We knew he was outside, but how did he get out? Surely zombies can't manoeuvre doors? We carried on towards the end of the corridor, we noticed light coming from the back door leading outside. It was a fire door so there shouldn't be as much light as we were seeing.

We quickly realised the door wasn't shut properly. Nick jumped into action and ran for the door. He stopped as we all saw a shadow move from one side of the door to the other, coming from the outside. He took the crowbar from me and held it up, readying himself for whatever was on the other side, and inched closer to the door. As soon as the door was in reach he yanked the handle and slammed it shut. Whatever was outside wasn't getting back in. We were terrified; we didn't want to be close to any of those things.

We went back to apartment 32; the door was left ajar. We stood outside a few moments listening for any movement from the inside. Nick slamming the door should have stirred anything nasty lurking on the inside. It was quiet, so we let ourselves in.

The smell was the first thing that hit us. It was a damp, rotting smell so powerful that we all had to take a step back. I took a deep breath whilst Nick and Andy pulled their shirts up to their noses, and we carried on inside.

In life, the old man must have been a hoarder. Cardboard boxes filled every nook and cranny; we had to step carefully to manoeuvre ourselves round.

"Mate, this place stinks, it's a complete mess!" Nick started.

"Eugh, you're telling me! Think we should just move on, it's full of shit. We're never gonna find anything," said Andy.

"No, we got this far, let's just see what we can take. Andy, you take that room," I said pointing, to the bedroom. "Nick, you take the living room and I'll head for the kitchen."

"I'm not eating anything that's come from that kitchen," Nick mumbled, disgusted by our surroundings.

I ignored them both; they were being childish. We needed to get supplies. We were low on food, water and had no weapons of any kind. Whilst Nick and Andy started sieving through the contents of the various boxes I made my way into the kitchen.

It was now obvious where the smell was coming from. Rotting vegetables covered the counter. Green liquid was seeping out the fridge. It had formed a sticky yellow pool on the floor. I heaved.

"You okay in there?" Nick shouted to me, hearing me retch.

"Yeah, I'm fine, just go look for stuff," I replied, eager to get this over with.

I pulled myself together. I started on checking the kitchen cupboards, looking for anything that hadn't expired. I managed to find a reusable Tesco bag, so I started putting the various cans I had found into it. I was able to find four cans of baked beans, a can of baby carrots, sweetcorn, tuna, a tin of spam and a tin of corned beef. I also found an unopened box of bran flakes and some cartons of fruit juice. It wasn't a massive haul, but at least it was something. At this point, anything we could get our hands on was greatly appreciated.

In the meantime, Nick and Andy were sifting through the mess trying to find something of use.

Nick had found a battered game of Monopoly, along with a chess set and Cluedo. Not very helpful in terms of survival, but at least it would give us something to do. He had also found bandages, prescription tablets and few old books. Not a great find, but the medical supplies were welcomed. We never knew when we might need them.

"Guys, come and look at this!" Andy shouted eagerly from the next room. We ran in to see what he had found.

He was stood inspecting a thick blade; it had an ivory handle, and the pouch was also cased in ivory. It was easily the size of a rhino horn. "Wait, there's more," he said, mesmerised.

He pointed to the bed. He had laid his findings across the edge of the bed. There were seven knives in total, all different shapes and sizes. Most had an African feel to them; most had some kind of tribal print. They looked like they hadn't been touched in years.

"He must have been a collector or hunter of some sorts," I pointed out. As we looked around the room, we saw all different types of African artefacts. There were tribal statues, canvas of intricately painted lions and zebras, pottery and tribal masks. All of which were covered in dust. They hadn't seen the light of day for a good few years.

"I think we better get this stuff upstairs," I said, wrapping up the various knives. "I think we've done well so far, let's get this stuff back up and regroup."

So far we had only taken small steps, but small steps such as these had enabled our survival so far. We didn't go out attacking all the infected we came across. We had to be tactical; our main aim was to stay safe and stay alive. We hadn't seen much action so far. If we had, I might not be alive to tell this tale.

After we had dropped our findings off in our apartment, we headed back downstairs. We were confident we had got what we could from Apartment 32, so Apartment 33 was next on the list.

"Let's see what's behind door number two," Nick joked as he jammed the crowbar into the door.

"Try not to hurt yourself," I responded, rolling my eyes.

When we finally got through the door, the apartment was evidentially more pleasant than the last. It belonged to a sweet old couple. I passed them a few times on the way to my car. They lived directly below us, although we never spoke.

The décor seemed considerably better than the last, but this one also had a strange smell. It had an unusual old people smell, mixed with rotting meat. Imagine how a raw chicken would smell after a week in the sun, covered in flies. That was exactly it.

We continued down the hallway towards the living area. As we opened the door to the living room, all was quiet.

Everything was intact, and for all intents and purposes it was completely liveable.

We split up to check the same rooms as last time.

I headed for the kitchen. Armed with my trusted Tesco bag, I started by opening the cupboards. The kitchen in this apartment was much nicer than the first.

Everything was in its rightful place; decorative plates covered the window sill, nothing was left out on the counter. The people that lived were obviously very house-proud.

The kitchen cupboards were presented immaculately. All the canned foods were stacked neatly, labels facing forward. Cereals lined one of the cupboards; each cereal variety was housed in its own Tupperware container keeping the food fresh.

I took everything I could get my hands on. It didn't take long to fill my bag completely.

Nick had been slightly more successful in this trip. He had found a full first aid kit along with a mass of various prescription pills.

As I walked through to the living room, armed with a weeks' worth of food I watched Nick as he stood with his arms folded, his hand resting under his chin. He looked deep in thought.

"What's up?" I asked snapping him out of his daydream.

"Trying to work out where these people have gone, babe; that's all," he replied, his posture never changing.

"Why are you so interested?" I pressed on.

"Well, the first aid kit here. Everything is there apart from what looks like a few large bandages." He pointed to an empty corner in the box. "This must have been used recently. When I found it, it was here on this table wide open."

"Okay, well done, Sherlock. But I'm still not following."

He shut the box. "Look, there's a bloody handprint on top of the box. One of them could have got infected. If so, where are they?"

"I honestly don't know," I replied. "But there's no use dwelling over it. Let's just grab what we can and move on. Can you carry the food back? It's heavy."

"Are you okay in there, Andy?" I shouted to the bedroom.

"Yeah, I'm fine, not a thing in here though. Just clothes and half an old blanket," came his reply. "I'm just going to check the bathroom, see if there's anything in there worth taking, and then I'm done too."

Half an old blanket? I thought to myself. How does that even work?

He wandered over to the bathroom; he opened the door and closed it again after only a couple of seconds. "Nothing in there. C'mon, let's go." His voice shook. He was suddenly very eager to get out the apartment.

I took one look at him, "Andy, what's in there?" I asked firmly.

"Nothing, let's just go," he said, dismissingly.

Nick and I looked at each other. We both made our way towards the bathroom door. We stood outside for a few seconds our ears pressed to the door.

When we were couldn't hear anything, Nick pushed the door open. We were both taken aback.

There, hanging from the shower pole over the bath, were two dead bodies. It was the old couple. By the looks of it, they had made their own nooses and hanged themselves. They must have thought that death was a far better option.

Unfortunately, shortly after hanging themselves, the virus must have kicked in. The couple hanging before us were moving. Their necks had clearly been broken and were completely bent out of place. However, this did not seem to faze them in the slightest. Black flies swarmed around them, landing all over their faces and in their eyes. Their skin was just as pale as the man we saw outside.

Seeing us stood in front of them must have excited them. They were fanatically moving their arms and legs, trying to get to us, not quite understanding they were stuck in mid-air.

The old woman opened her mouth; she tried to let out a screech but, instead, black blood poured out her mouth and down her front. She stared straight at me. Her cold, dead eyes bore into mine. I was frozen in fear. The small was ungodly, though it barely registered with me.

The sight was horrific. Nick closed the door quickly. Andy was already springing into action. He had raced into the living room and was currently attempting to manoeuvre an armchair in front of the bathroom door.

Nick turned and left to help him while I went searching for a knife. The old couple had the same type of lock on their bathroom door as we did upstairs. The lock was easily overridden from the outside by a coin or a knife.

As soon as I found a knife I ran over and turned the lock. The boys pushed the armchair against the door even as we heard a loud thud from the inside of the bathroom.

"Shit, one of them must have got loose," I speculated.

We grabbed our findings and shot out the apartment, slamming the door as best we could on our way out.

As soon as we got back upstairs we immediately barricaded the door back up. Duckface, seeing our urgency, put her fingers to her lips, and without saying a word helped us to barricade the door back up, placing each item against the door as carefully as possible. We all followed suit. Not quite knowing why we had to be so quiet.

Once the barricade was up we all walked into the living room, where the curtains were still drawn.

"I think we've attracted some unwanted attention," Duckface explained. "I've been checking out the windows while you've been gone, more and more keep turning up. I've stayed out of sight, but they keep coming," she said, her voice trembling.

I got up and went over to the bay window. Staying out of sight, I peered through the side of the curtain.

The street outside seemed a lot more active than it had ever been. I counted twenty infected in total. So far they didn't know we were here and had not attempted to get into our building. I went into the kitchen to check the back; there were eight of them milling around, three of them were scratching on the back door. This worried me even more.

"The noise we made downstairs must have stirred them up," Nick speculated. "The good news is we have more supplies, we're still safe here and we have more food. That should last us about a week."

We explained to Duckface what had happened in the old couple's apartment. We told her that for now they couldn't get out. How long it would hold them was anyone's guess.

We needed to come up with a plan. It was now far too dangerous for us to go outside, and we had no idea what was lurking in the apartments next to us – or above.

Chapter 5

Making a Plan

"Oh God, what are we going to do?" Duckface whined. "There's those things out there and in here, now?" Her high pitched whinge went straight through me.

"I don't know, we need to be sensible about this. If we leave here where are we going to go? And how are we going to get out?" I replied, cutting her off before she had a chance to carry on.

"What about our family and friends? I need to see if my parents are okay, and my sister," Andy said seemingly worried.

"So do I, my mum and my sister are out there somewhere," I agreed.

Nick took the lead. "We all have family we want to get to, but we need to think about us too. We need to keep ourselves alive; I'm not saying we don't try and find them. But we need to make sure we stay safe, I'm not risking my life on the off chance they may or may not be there. If we're sure there's little danger, then yes, but if there's loads of them out there, I'm not risking it," he said, pointing outside.

We sat there for a few minutes thinking, none of us said anything. We certainly needed a plan. We couldn't stay in the apartment forever. It was getting more and more dangerous as the number of infected increased.

Duckface grabbed her phone. "I'm going to check my page, see if anyone's been on lately." It was becoming clear her role was the communicator of the group.

We were all doing what we could. The boys were the brawn; they did the heavy lifting and more dangerous tasks not officially meant for girls.

I took on the supply inventory. I was the cook in the group so I knew exactly how long our food would last and was able to come up with ways of making it last longer, combining different ingredients.

Myself and Nick seemed to be the leaders. We had the most common sense – and the best survival instincts, it seemed. We were already starting to work together as a unit, without even thinking about it.

"I think it would be a good idea if we each packed an emergency bag and left it by the door. If something bad was to happen and we needed to leave in a hurry, we won't have time to pack," I suggested. We needed to be prepared for every eventuality.

We all agreed this was a good idea, so I went about trying to find some suitable bags. After going through my wardrobes the best I could come up with were two decent-sized Louis

Vuitton leather weekender bags. I handed one to Duckface and kept the other for myself. They weren't the most practical, but they were a good size, and at least we would still go out in style.

I checked through Nick's wardrobes and came across a Nike sports bag and an old Fila backpack. These looked much more suitable, so I handed them to the boys.

I made everyone a list of what to pack. It was best that everyone took their own supplies in case one of the bags got lost or compromised. The list was as follows:

2 x changes of clothes
1 x hoody/coat
1 x pair of sensible shoes
1 x make-up wipes
1 x pair of gloves
1 x blanket
1 x sharp knife (wrapped in a pillowcase)
1 x set of cutlery
1 x lighter
1 x first aid kit
2 x bottles of water
4 x cans of food

I also added items for each person to carry. These included a can opener, crowbar, wind-up torch, various tools, weapons, shampoo, shower gel, biscuits and juice.

I quickly grabbed mine and Nick's passports at the last minute.

Granted it wasn't a lot, but it was all we had in the apartment. Once the bags were packed Nick started to put the bags by the door. He started pulling out all his fishing gear and piled it up with the bags.

"Babe, what are you doing with all your fishing stuff out?" I asked.

"Well, if we go out on the road, we don't know where we'll end up. If it comes to it, I know where all the rivers and lakes are. If we're short of food we may need to use it."

The number of bags seemed impractical, but he was right. It may save our lives. There was a lot of stuff, but we should be just about able to carry it.

Saying that, I was surprised at him. I have never known anyone hate fish as much as he does. He loves fishing but has always refused to eat it. It never made sense to me at all. Why fish if you have no intention of eating it? I saw no point to it whatsoever. As they say, desperate times call for desperate measures.

We carried on planning our escape route. We had decided when we left we would take two cars; at least if something happened to one, we could all hop into the other. We decided to take my car and Andy's. Andy's car was a Mazda CX-5 in blue. It was a crossover so it had good boot space and was fairly economical. It would get us a fair distance as long as we reserved fuel. My car was a white Nissan Qashqai. It was the bigger of the two but again was fairly economical. Both these cars were very sturdy so they seemed the safest options. Luckily both cars had nearly a full tank of fuel.

We had agreed to wait a couple more days before planning an escape. We wanted to wait for the crowd of infected to go down and leave the area. Whilst they were outside we studied them. We needed to know how they reacted and how they interacted with others. We knew very little about the virus or the effect it had on its hosts.

Over the next couple of days we took turns sitting by the window; we kept a journal of all our findings, at least it was something to keep us occupied. We watched them round the clock, for hours at a time. Some of them stared into space, others walked around aimlessly, some walked following a set path. None of us could make any sense of them. They didn't seem to sleep, and their movements seemed sluggish and clumsy. Half the time it was like watching a child walk for the first time. They all had the same pale complexion. Some had gaping wounds, which would render the living incapacitated. That's how I knew they were dead. Blood no longer flowed from the wounds, yet the wounds had not scabbed. Some of the infected who had passed by had missing limbs. This did not seem to faze them in the slightest.

I watched one infected man walk carefully around each car and stop and stare into the road. He looked like a parking warden the way he was inspecting each car as he passed them, so I named him Walter the warden.

Boredom was getting the better of all of us. We spent countless hours playing Monopoly and Cluedo. In each game of Monopoly, I ended up severely bankrupting every other player, but after a while even winning started to get boring.

Andy and Nick had taken up playing chess; they both got really into it, and were always highly competitive.

"Tell you what we would go nicely with this game," Andy said halfway through one of their many chess games, "a nice glass of Hennessy Brandy – vintage of course."

"More of a whisky man myself," Nick added, advancing his way to Andy's Queen. "Glenfiddich single malt, on the rocks."

"God, you two sound like such old men! Get a grip," I interrupted, stopping them before they drooled over the chess board.

"It's a man thing," Duckface added. "Wouldn't mind a nice glass of Pinot Noir," she carried on.

"Sounds simple, but a hot shower would make me happy," I added.

We spent the next few hours reminiscing of the old days, the days before the virus took over. We talked about holidays we had been on, places we'd visited and happy memories we shared.

For the first time in a long time, we were all getting along well. We laughed and joked with each other; it was starting to feel like the good old days.

We were brought back to reality by an almighty thud emanating from the guest room. We ran in to find out where the noise was coming from. It was the other side of the wall that we shared with our neighbour.

It was a constant bang, as if someone was punching the wall trying to break their way through.

The noise from inside was stirring up the infected outside. They became more animated, looking around trying to figure out where the sound was coming from. They gradually made their way towards our building. They made no attempt to open the doors, yet they started banging on the doors in time to the bangs that could be heard from next door.

It was as if they were somehow communicating with one another. We were surrounded. Both our exits out the building were blocked. The banging was now going on all around us, perfectly in sync.

We heard the glass downstairs smash, yet still the banging continued.

"What are they doing?" Duckface whispered, her voice shaking. We were all huddled together on the living room floor. We stayed away from the windows, not wanting to make our presence known.

"Do they know we're here or something?" she asked, trying to make sense of it all. I had no idea what was going on around us. None of it made sense. What could they possibly gain from this?

Nick got up and went to check out the window in our bedroom, it directly faced the entrance door outside. He came back after a few minutes. "They're not attempting to get in at all. The glass smashed over the door, and they've moved away from it, if they wanted to get in they could easily climb through." He looked at us all completely baffled. "They're just banging on the walls and windows, just making noise."

We all looked at one another. We needed to stay as quiet as possible. We knew hardly anything about the things outside.

We didn't know how clever they were, how long they would live or how they communicated if they even communicated at all.

The only things we knew about them were from what we observed. They moved very slowly and seemed slow to react. Walter the warden was the only one of them that seemed to have any sense, if you could even call it that. Between us, we had limited experience, only a few of us had been within a close proximity of them, and we had all been able to avoid close combat.

We sat on the living room floor for hours, holding onto our partners. We were silent. The only noises that could be heard were the on-going bangs from around the building.

We were all terrified. I grabbed onto Nick, burying my head in his chest trying to block out the sound. What the hell were they doing? This didn't seem normal at all. I kept racking my brains trying to come up with a logical explanation for all of this. But there was no explanation, at least not yet.

After a couple of hours, the banging died down. Within two minutes it went from full on banging on the walls to complete silence. We looked out the window. The infected had all gone back to wandering around the streets, exactly as they were before the banging started. It was as if nothing happened. Their behaviour was baffling.

Nothing could be heard at all from the inside; however, we had made a unanimous decision to stay clear of next door. Whatever supplies we needed, they weren't worth risking our lives for. Whatever it was next door, it was going to stay there.

"I don't understand," I whispered, "why spend hours banging on the doors but make no attempt to go inside?"

"I know, I don't get it either," Duckface agreed.

"Maybe they're just trying to scare us," said Andy. "Who knows if they're that clever, but it's the only thing I can think of."

"You might be right, but I don't want to sit around here and find out. We're like fish in a barrel here," Nick replied.

Duckface interjected, "I've been checking over my page; a few people have said a shelter has been set up in Woodford. It's safe, and there's food and water, what do you guys think?"

"I don't know, sounds like a good idea but it depends on who's there. More people will attract more of those things," Andy replied.

"I'm not sure who, but people have said they making their way there. Has to be better than this, it's at the old airfield," Duckface replied.

"Okay, we're going to have to leave sooner or later. If there's a chance, I say we take it." For once I found myself agreeing with Duckface. "We already have our bags packed. Let's wait until we see an opening, and we'll go."

We all agreed; we needed to wait for the opportune moment. There were still around twenty infected wandering about outside. Their behaviour already had me on edge.

We decided to leave the next day, as early as possible. After observing the infected, they seemed to be less active first thing. We spent our last evening deep in thought. We barely spoke to one another. After spending so much time together in such close quarters, we had run out of things to say.

After having an early night, we all got up that morning at six a.m. After we got changed and un-barricaded the door, we took a quick look outside. The atmosphere outside was surreal; clouds covered the whole of the sky, it was a typical September morning. The grass was damp with dew, and a cold breeze ran through the trees. There were only three of the infected left outside; they were at the opposite end of the car park. As far as we were aware, the coast was clear.

We grabbed our bags and carefully made our way outside. Glass sat in a pile at the bottom of the stairs; we carefully stepped over it, trying not to make any noise. My car was directly outside the door, which was easy for me and Nick. Duckface and Andy had a bit further to walk, but the infected hadn't seen us yet, so we had time.

As soon as we got outside the three remaining infected turned to us, alerted to our presence. They started making their way towards us. As they started to move we noticed more coming out from all around us, at least four were by the side of the building; another five came out from the street opposite us. One even came out from behind the oak tree.

If I didn't know any better, I could have sworn they were waiting for us. We all stood looking at each and every one of them as they marched towards us. They seemed more eager than usual; they picked up their pace considerably, compared to the last encounters I had with them. They were almost speed walking.

We all raced to our cars; I got in the driver's seat as Nick threw the bags in the back. He ran round the car, into the passenger's seat, just as I heard the first bang against the car. As soon as he closed the door I slammed on the locks.

I fumbled putting the keys into the ignition, praying that the car would start. As soon as the car sprang to life I threw my gears into reverse as I backed over one of the infected. There were more making their way towards us, at least thirty of them now, closing in from all different directions.

I looked over to Duckface and Andy to check they had made their way to the car okay. There were five infected all around their car, vigorously banging on the doors and windows, trying to seek purchase on their prizes they had waited so patiently for.

Just as I had, Andy threw his car into reverse; the infected stumbled trying to regain their balance as both cars shot off into the distance.

Chapter 6

The Flight Path

Our route was easy enough. It was a straight road to get us there, besides Woodford wasn't known for being a well-populated area. It was full of grand houses, set far back from the road. Woodford was an expensive place to live; all the houses must have had at least five bedrooms and multiple bathrooms. The houses were stunning.

As we made our way to the airfield, the roads seemed dead. No one could be seen or heard. We had to weave our way through a multitude of abandoned cars, which were blocking the road ahead.

As we neared the airfield, we saw a large crowd gathering outside. There must have been at least fifty of the infected pressing against the chain link fence, separating the airfield from the main road.

The entrance to the airfield originally had an automatic arm barrier. By the looks of it, it had been reinforced, as now a twenty foot tall steel gate stood towering in its place.

We peered out the car window, trying to sneak a closer look. We saw a military 4x4 with a machine-gun turret strapped to the back, along with some sort of canvas covered carrier lorry. The guns looked very intimidating. They army must have had this place well under control.

There were no signs of survivors or the military, but we felt confident they were inside.

We stopped the cars about a hundred yards down the road. It was clear we wouldn't be able to gain access through the entrance. There were far too many of the infected outside, even if we did get in, we would end up letting a few of the infected pass through the gates. We knew that it simply wasn't an option.

We turned around, as Nick suggested we take a detour down Old Hall Lane instead. As we turned into the road, I saw an old church and a large graveyard on our right-hand side. There was a blue sign on the corner that read WELCOME TO CHRIST CHURCH. A restaurant I had passed many times stood opposite. Both buildings had an eerie feel to them. We could not see or hear a single person, so we carried on our journey.

The further we drove into Old Hall Lane, the narrower the road became. As we pushed forward it became a single-lane road. Hedgerows blocked our view on either side as the smooth tarmac disappeared. The road soon turned into an extremely bumpy dirt track. We swerved many times just to avoid the countless potholes.

Eventually, the hedgerows disappeared as the road curved to the left, revealing a warehouse-sized barn, made from brick and corrugated metal. There were two openings to the barn – both had green metal doors. The smaller door of the two looked like it had been kicked through revealing part of the framework within the door. I still couldn't see any sign of life; it was deathly silent.

We carried on past the farmhouse and various outbuildings. As we passed a farm, fields opened up on our left-hand side, spanning for miles. We searched for an opening in the airfield, but it was still all fenced off. I felt my previous optimism begin to drain. The threat of the infected seemed minimal, but if we couldn't get in, then this place would be useless to us. I hoped to God we hadn't left the security of our apartment for nothing.

We drove up to an old rusty gate. Hanging from it was a green sign with yellow writing that read 'Keep Clear Emergency Exit Number 1' the gate had chains wrapping around both gates: no one was getting in through there. We carried on going, luck was not on our side. A few yards down the road and we came to Woodford Golf Club. Cars were parked in a small car park, but still no one could be seen. The whole place had been abandoned.

We pulled up next to the golf club. There, across the road, was another rusty gate with the same sign as before 'Keep Clear Emergency Exit Number 2'.

We got out of the cars for a closer inspection. Although the gate was closed, it was unlocked. Nick and I left the confides of our car to take a closer look. We were in luck, Nick began to open the gate as I got back into the car. As soon as we had both cars through the gate and into the airfield Nick secured the gate and jumped back in.

"Where the hell do we go now?" I asked him looking around at the vast amount of runway laid out before me. There were many outbuildings and hangars leading off in all different directions. This whole place was a minefield.

Nick pointed straight ahead. "Let's try that one, it looks safe enough, and it's far enough away from the entrance that if those things get in, we'll have some time to escape."

I agreed and him, so we drove towards the hanger. Both cars did a lap of the building, as we tried to find a way in. From first inspection, it didn't look like anyone was around; we were about to give up and check the next building when we heard the sound of metal shaking and parting. We drove back around to the front. There were two men in military uniforms on either side of the door, ushering us in.

As we pulled in, the light from inside the hangar blinded us. The whole of the interior was painted a brilliant white, even the floor. Sat in the middle was a large, impressive plane. It was a large jet, glistening white. It looked brand new. The side of the plane read Airbus A350 Prestige. The door was open on the front right hand side with steps leading up to the door.

We pulled up opposite the plane and cautiously opened the doors. The two men were walking towards us, in full combat gear, each cradling an automatic rifle barrel-down with an air of professional confidence. I already felt much safer just being in their presence.

"Good morning. My name is Flight Sergeant Jeff Tanner, and this is my second in command Corporal Ryan Jameson."

"Hi," I replied weakly. The sergeant was a middle-aged man; he wore a navy blazer which accentuated his broad shoulders, underneath he had a black tie and sky blue shirt, all in pristine condition. He stood with his hat tucked underneath his arm. His whole demeanour seemed to command respect. He was a man of authority.

His corporal had the same posture and uniform, yet he seemed to have a younger and kinder face. He reminded me of Captain America. He was incredibly good-looking – he just had a certain look about him. He had short blond hair and blue eyes. He smiled as he shook our hands, and we locked eyes for what felt like minutes.

The sergeant continued. "Please do not be alarmed; we wish you no harm. We are responsible for base security. There aren't many of us anymore. We can provide you with shelter, food and water. Our main base was compromised, so we have been positioned here for the last week. We have a lot to discuss, please come this way."

We looked at one another, equally confused, but followed the sergeant as he led the way. "When the outbreak first hit Europe we reopened the airbase, under the command of the Ministry of Defence. We were positioned here to provide support to the British Army, and to help prevent the spread of infection."

"So where's everyone now?" Nick asked as we walked around the back of the plane.

"When the outbreak hit the capital, the majority of our squad were redeployed to the Midlands, to try and stop the outbreak on its journey north." The sergeant continued: "I was put in command of the remaining personnel as we continued to establish a containment area. This whole airbase had been designed as a safe haven; our aim was to use this area as a refuge, a safe place for survivors."

He stopped when we reached the far wall of the hangar where wooden crates lined the wall. Next to the crates were multiple gas canisters. "These crates are filled with MREs. This stands for Meals, Ready-to Eat'. They have been used in the Army for years now. They aren't the most appetising foods in the world. But they are substantial."

"If this is a safe place, then where are the rest of the survivors?" I asked, thinking that clearly something wasn't adding up.

"Our main base was the building towards the entrance. Within the base we established living quarters, a canteen, showering facilities and a medical centre. Shortly after the infection reached us here, we started to take in more and more casualties. The MoD had warned us not to take in any survivors who had been bitten or seemed to be contracting a fever; however, they refused to tell us why. We followed our orders at first. After a few days, a private brought a young boy to my attention. He was only four years of age. He had a small bite. The private explained to me he had been bitten by his mother and that he couldn't leave him behind."

I looked at the sergeant, understanding where the rest of this story was going.

"I made an exception for the little boy and sent him to the medical wing, where he developed a fever and infection. After four hours, the boy was pronounced dead. Within fifteen minutes of death, the boy reanimated. He started feeding on the other survivors, who then infected my men. I had no choice but to lock the whole building down. The corporal and I were on the other side of the air base when I got the call. I made the decision there and then."

The sergeant looked to the floor, shaking his head.

The corporal spoke up: "You see, it wasn't just the survivors and our men that were in there, our families were there too."

I looked closer at the two men standing before us. Beneath the military exterior, I could see the pain in their eyes. They were both family men at heart. Although their job was to serve our country, they lived for their family. For the first time since the virus took over, I felt lucky. Although I didn't have my family, I had my fiancé; he was my future family. I squeezed his hand tighter.

"I'm so sorry. You made the right decision. If you hadn't, the chances are you wouldn't be here today," I told them.

"Shall we continue with our tour?" the corporal asked us all, lightening the mood.

We followed them to the other side of the building, where the flight sergeant stopped outside two metal double doors. There was an electronic keypad on the side of the wall. "We used this particular hangar to store supplies. You've already seen our food supply? Well, that's not the only thing we kept here."

Punching in the code, the flight sergeant opened the doors. "This is our ammunition store," he announced.

All the walls inside were steel. Lining each wall were a range of guns varying from assault rifles, submachine guns and pistols. I even spotted my favourite gun of all time: a Barrett 50 cal. Boxes of ammunition lined the room, all different shapes and sizes. Grenades and knives were laid out on multiple tables circling the room.

"Only Corporal Jameson and I have the code for this room, so the only rule I have in this hangar is that no one enters this room without myself or Corporal Jameson here."

We nodded; it was fair enough. We were just grateful they had let us in.

"As you can see we are very well equipped, we try not to use any weapon unless we need to. There is more to see, but for now, would you like to see your living quarters?" the corporal asked.

He led us to the plane. The flight sergeant went into the plane first while his corporal stood by and let us all past.

"This plane has been here since we took over the base. We tried to trace the owner, however the company say it is simply in storage, it has yet to be sold. Given the current circumstances, I don't think there will be any buyers any time soon."

We looked around the entrance. Cream carpets lined the floors, velvet curtains separated each section of the plane.

"Let me introduce you to your fellow survivors," the flight sergeant advised as he opened the first velvet curtain.

As we entered the cabin, we noticed a long, leather sofa curving around the room. Adjacent to the sofa sat four stools along a wooden veneer bar. There were three people sat on the curving sofa. One was an elderly man named George, the other two we all knew very well.

Lacey and her husband Paul were here too. They were both very good friends of ours. Paul and Nick were practically inseparable. Lacey and I had been friends for a long time; we started out as work colleagues and rapidly became close friends.

Lacey was sat with a huge grin on her face. She still had a glowing complexion, her tan still visible from their recent holiday in the Maldives. It was strange seeing her without make-up on; her hair was tied up in a bun and she was dressed for comfort. She was very much like me before the virus took over. She lived her life in heels; she was always very glamorous. Her long red hair was always perfect – she never had a hair out of place. She was quite tall, without her heels she was pushing five foot seven. She had lovely green eyes; she was the type of person that couldn't do enough for you. She was one of my closest friends.

Her husband Paul was also smiling. He had his arm placed over her shoulder and his eyes lit up when he saw us. He too seemed to be dressed very casually. He was a businessman. Thinking back, I can't remember the last time I saw him without a suit on. Like Lacey, he was very tall. He stood at a whopping six foot four. He had a slim figure, although he detested working out. How he managed to stay in shape was a mystery to us all. They complemented each other perfectly. They never boasted or spoke about their relationship, but you could tell they were still so in love. They were the happiest couple I had ever met.

We perked up the second we saw them and ran over to greet them. Duckface and Andy stayed back. We were all close friends at one point; however the relationship between Duckface and Lacey soon became sour. Inevitably I ended up stuck in the middle as the other two constantly feuded.

There were no bad feelings between any of the boys as they were happily talking amongst themselves.

Duckface and Lacey made no attempt to communicate with each other at all. Sensing the tension, the corporal interrupted. "I take it you all know each other? I will show each of you your living quarters, and then we shall all get better acquainted."

Jameson took Duckface and Andy to their room whilst the flight sergeant ushered Nick and me to ours. We followed the flight sergeant up the stairs towards the back of the plane, which revealed another floor. He opened the door to the first room on the left. "We were very fortunate to find this plane, I'm sure you will all agree our surroundings are rather luxurious," he announced.

"This is stunning." I was in awe as I walked in. A double bed stood in the middle of the room; the bed was perfectly made and was covered in elegant, intricately detailed gold cushions. A small mirrored wardrobe sat facing the side of the bed with a small walkway in between.

"It's not the biggest room in the world, but it's the best we can offer," the flight sergeant explained. "If you could follow me, I shall show you the dining room. We eat all our meals together. I think it's important have at least one group meal together a day. Right now we are all family. We are all we have. Each individual is as important as the next; I think it's important we all keep this in mind." He had clearly aimed the last part at Duckface who had joined us in the dining room along with Andy and the corporal.

"I will now leave you to get better acquainted; I believe you have some old friends who I'm sure have got a lot to tell. Corporal, I trust I can leave you to look after our new guests and make them feel at home?"

The corporal nodded.

"I will take the first watch, I look forward to getting to know each of you." The two military men stiffened to attention before the flight sergeant walked off, leaving us with the corporal.

"You guys must be hungry, can I get you some lunch? I can teach you how these MREs work. As the flight sergeant said, they're not the most appealing but they do the job."

"Sounds good, I'm starving," Nick complained. I could tell he was feeling more himself, food was always the first thing on his mind.

As we headed back downstairs, I noticed Duckface hung back. It wasn't just that she didn't want to be around Lacey, I knew she was scared of her. Lacey always spoke her mind, which is what I always liked about her. She was always truthful and wouldn't stand for snobbery. She had no problem in being confrontational, but she was always fair.

Her husband Paul was a few years older than us; he was in his mid-thirties. He had a very good job which meant they were both able to live comfortably. If I'm honest, I think the main reason she and Duckface fell out was because Duckface was jealous of her lifestyle. She always felt the need to one-up Lacey; it was like a bragging contest between them both on who earned the most.

The boys followed Jameson to the other side of the plane as I went into the bar area, to have a much needed catch up with Lacey, whilst Duckface took herself off to bed.

"I can't believe you're here, what happened?" I asked, trying to make sense of today's events.

"We were really lucky, hun, we stayed at home the day it started. Paul was going to leave for the office, but I begged him not to go. Finally, he decided to stay. We saw on the news what was going on and locked all the doors. We were safe for a couple of days, but then those things started coming in through into the garden. We knew we would be surrounded soon, so we grabbed the keys and ran for the car."

I looked at her completely shocked. "Did you not take anything with you?"

Lacey shook her head.

"We completely panicked, we left everything behind."

"So how did you end up here?" I asked.

"Well, we got in the car and we drove. We didn't know where to go. We pulled over to the side of the road as soon as we were clear, to get our heads straight. It was then we saw an army truck driving past. We decided to follow it; we didn't know what else to do. We followed them here, and they took us in."

I was so relieved they made it here okay. I would much rather have spent the three weeks trapped in the apartment with Lacey and Paul than Duckface and Andy, who we ended up lumbered with. I'll admit, I liked the fact Lacey and Duckface hated each other so much, I completely agreed with Lacey, and it inevitably brought us closer. At least I wasn't the only one who didn't like her.

"So what happened to you then? How come you ended up with them?" she whispered.

I recounted the events that happened, from the incident on the factory floor all the way up to our escape from the apartment.

"Wow, I can't believe you had to spend that long with her. I would have slapped her and kicked her out. You're too nice for your own good."

The conversation soon changed; it was like the old days, when we used to spend hours giggling over a bottle of wine or two.

Duckface stayed locked away in her room, we both preferred it that way. I had spent way too long in her company, and I think if Lacey never saw her again, it would be too soon.

Before long the boys came in, each had two pans in their hands. They looked very proud of themselves. The food, unfortunately, did not look very appealing. I felt like a parent having to pretend to eat mud pie, whilst rubbing my stomach and saying 'mmmm'.

Flight sergeant Tanner came in for lunch. Shortly after we had all finished Jameson switched places to take watch.

"Now I know you haven't had much time to settle in here, however I must insist we get down to business," the flight sergeant announced.

We all looked at him intrigued as to what he wanted from us. I was still unsure.

"We have all managed to survive for this long. But there is a difference between surviving and living." He carried on, "I would like to find more survivors. I believe we should help anyone we can. My men could be in the same situation as we are, each hanger on this airbase served a different purpose, although the main base was compromised, I do not yet know what the others hold. I owe it to my men to find them, and I want your help with that."

"But how can we do anything?" I asked. "I don't understand what you want from us?"

"I believe that each individual has their own strengths and weaknesses. I do not yet know what they are, but I have no doubt in my mind that each and every one of you have something to contribute."

Nick spoke up. "I for one am very grateful for your hospitality, we would all be struggling out there if you hadn't of let us in. Anything I can do to help, I will."

"That is very good to hear, thank you for your support Nick. If I may be so bold –the vehicles you came in with, they will help with our mission greatly."

"So you want to use our cars?" I pressed.

"Yes, with your permission, of course. Now I will of course ensure both your vehicles are topped up at all times, we have an array of military vehicles stored along with a built-up gas pump in one of these hangars, which is my main priority. But until we get to them, your vehicles would be a great help to us."

"Okay, that's fine by me Sergeant, but on one condition. I'd like you to teach me how to use the weapons in there." I pointed to the ammunition store.

"I have a pretty good shot, but my experience is limited to air rifles. I know I can handle myself, and I want to be able to defend myself. In fact, I think all of us do."

"That's an interesting proposal, let me think about that. Right now, I think its best we all rest up; I think it's safe to say you have had a pretty stressful day. Try and forget about it for now. We will all talk more in the morning."

It was all very strange; we had barely been here two minutes and the flight sergeant already had plans for us. I wasn't completely sure how much I trusted him.

We spent the rest of that day talking, sharing experiences, looking back on the days before the infection. We almost forgot what was happening in the world around us. It was refreshing being in the company of new people, somehow the world seemed a little bigger than what we were used to. The fact that no one was sat round playing on their phones was alien to me; we spent all night talking to each other, face to face. No texting, Facebooking or tweeting, it was strangely liberating.

I spent a few hours talking to our other fellow survivor, George. He was the airfield manager. He was assisting the RAF when the infection came. No one knew the way around the hangar the way George did. He even told me about a few secret passageways in and around the base, which had been built around the time of the First World War.

He was a very interesting man. He told me he was seventy-six and still had no intention of giving up his job. Ever since he was a little boy he was obsessed with flying, he joined the RAF at a young age and before long he was training to be a pilot. He was one of the first pilots to be deployed in the Falklands War. He spent his time on the RAF Ascension Island airbase, flying Avro Vulcan B Mk 2 Bombers. Like the others, he was a military man. Even in his old age, he was very switched on. Once he reached retirement, he and his wife moved to the Woodford area. The airfield brought him back a lot of memories; it was where he felt most at home.

"So if you've flown planes before, why can't you fly this one?" I asked intrigued.

"My dear, planes nowadays are a lot different to the planes I flew back then. I can't get my head around these new fancy gadgets. This is a corporate jet – as much as I wish I could; it's not an option, I'm sorry."

It was a long shot. The flight sergeant came in and sat with us after overhearing our conversation.

"It's not just flying the plane that's the problem. There is no fuel in the tank, we have jet fuel on site, but even if we refilled successfully, we don't yet know where we would go. There are more important things we need to establish first, before making any rash decisions. I can assure you; we're safe here for now."

A few days after we had settled in, the Flight Sergeant Tanner called us all in for a meeting.

He spoke first. "Corporal Jameson and I have been discussing the possibility of training you all how to use weapons effectively. This goes against everything we have been trained, however giving the circumstances I believe it's the right thing to do."

Corporal Jameson stood up, addressing us all. "We will train you how to use weapons. But it's not just about shooting effectively. If you want to learn how to shoot, you must also learn how to survive."

Flight Sergeant Tanner continued: "We will train you all how to stay alive. That includes fitness, stealth, hand-to-hand combat, and most importantly working together.

"Now I won't force anybody to participate who does not wish to, however I will need an answer from you all now. Those not willing to take part can earn your keep in a different manner."

Andy was the first to speak up. "I'm in!" Paul and Nick soon followed suit.

Me and Lacey looked at each other and nodded. "Yes, we're in too."

This left only Duckface and George.

George spoke up. "I have already done my training, and I've served my time. If needs be, I know my way around a firearm. I'm too old for the training to be of any use, but I am happy to share my expertise."

"That would be much appreciated, sir," the flight sergeant replied, nodding his head to his senior, a sign of respect.

Duckface was quiet. We all stared at her, waiting for a response.

"Sorry, but I'm not going to do it. I don't feel comfortable around guns, and I don't agree with fighting. I'm not going to get involved with any of it," she snarled.

"Typical." Lacey rolled her eyes and glared at her.

"Well, I apologise for not wanting to stoop to your level. It's not right, and I refuse to have someone else's blood on my hands. You're all doing it now, so I don't have to. I don't see why I need to help anyway," she scoffed.

"To stay alive?" I asked. "To help and protect everyone here? I don't know, maybe even as a thank you to these men for taking us in? Shall I go on?"

"If you'd rather die" Lacey hit back, "then I'm more than happy to have your blood on my hands. At least you could come in useful for target practice, would be much better than you sitting on your arse all day. Waste of space."

"Of course I am," Duckface snorted sarcastically. "You don't even deserve to be here."

"Girls, please," Tanner said, stepping in. "Lola, if you don't want to take part you don't have to. However, we all need to start working together as a unit. Although I can appreciate you are not keen on weaponry. I do expect you to help in other ways."

She reluctantly agreed. "Fine."

Ignoring her less than receptive response, he addressed each of us. "As part of your training I expect each of you to help. You will be put on watch duty, learn to keep your weapons clean and will maintain a tight fitness regime. This may seem a little over the top, but you will learn to always be prepared for every eventuality. I want you all up at five a.m. sharp tomorrow morning, no exceptions." With that, he turned sharply and walked off.

Duckface quickly followed him out. Everyone started talking excitedly among themselves. Lacey and I stayed put.

"She may be good for target practice, as long as she shrank that massive head of hers. I don't think we could miss, even if we were blindfolded," I laughed.

"I don't know how he expects her to help, she's fucking useless," Lacey replied, a little louder than usual.

The feud between Duckface and Lacey had been going on for a long time. However, we were all inseparable at one point. She wasn't always the Duckface we see now. When we first met Lola she was a slightly geeky, naïve but sweet girl. She didn't have many friends, but the ones she had she kept close at heart. She would always do what she could for others, she never put herself first.

Things changed just before she met Andy. She had made some new friends through work and was going out with them more often. This didn't faze me or Lacey in the slightest; we were happy she was branching out and making new friends.

The more she started making new friends, the more she started to change. She started to become self-obsessed, caring more and more about the way she looked. It didn't just stop there; her whole attitude was completely different. She started referring to her new friends as 'the gang' taking every opportunity to explain to us that they don't let 'just anyone' into 'the gang' and how amazing it was that she was always invited out to social events. We didn't think anything of it at first. We were both a lot more established in our careers than she was, so we had more important things to concentrate on.

To be honest, we thought it all sounded a bit childish and were past the days where appearances ruled our lives. We were happy she was happy and let her get on with it. We were still supportive, and she still came to us when she needed advice.

As time went on she got a lot more self-involved, she was only interested about talking about herself, and spent more and more time bragging about how popular she was becoming, and how (according to her) all men were falling at her feet. Unfortunately, this was not the case at all. As soon as she opened her mouth, her whole life story came spewing out. We witnessed this on numerous occasions when we had gone out with her. It was cringe worthy. Men that originally approached her, after hearing her life story, ran a mile. She expected every man she came into contact with to fall at her feet and worship her. When this didn't happen, she became even more self-absorbed.

After she had met Andy, the dynamics changed again. She made the poor guy's life a misery; she became extremely possessive and flew off the handle on numerous occasions. She was starting to be embarrassing to go out with. After they had been dating for a while, he introduced her to his friends and their girlfriends. She was in her element; she made even more friends and her ego began to grow.

The problem was, the more time she spent with Andy's new friends, the less she spent with 'the gang'. After a few weeks, she went from talking about them constantly to never mentioning them at all. To her 'the gang' had served its purpose and were no longer needed. She stopped contacting them and never saw them again.

She was becoming more and more opinionated as time went on, using phrases like "I don't associate myself with those types of people." She became very two faced. She would talk about different friends behind their backs, but when they were face to face it was as if butter wouldn't melt. She was a completely different person.

Lacey and I both saw the drastic change in her. She seemed to thrive on drama, I caught her out a few times, lying and making up rumours I knew full well weren't true. I decided to cut her out and let her get on with her new life; I didn't want to be a part of it. I had made the decision to be civil to her as Andy and Nick got on well, and I didn't want to affect their friendship. As far as I was concerned our friendship was over.

Lacey, on the other hand, decided to confront her about her behaviour, in the hope that she would change her ways. Unfortunately, it didn't go quite according to plan.

Lacey arranged to see her and sit her down to air her concerns. Once Lacey had explained how she was feeling and the reasons why she felt as she did, she didn't get the reaction she was expecting. Duckface flew into a rage, telling Lacey that she was jealous because she didn't have many friends as she did and that Lacey just wanted her to herself. She even had the cheek to say that if she wanted, she could 'have' Paul. She told her that she was jealous of her because she and Andy were so well matched.

Lacey couldn't believe it. She kicked her out and refused to talk to her again. Not that I could blame Lacey in the slightest; I would have done the same thing if it'd been me.

That was the last encounter they had with each other before they met on the plane.

Chapter 7

Boot Camp

We were woken up the next morning by Corporal Jameson banging on our doors.

"C'mon, get up you lazy bastards we've got work to do, I want you all out this plane *now*!" He ordered.

We groggily pulled back the covers, got changed and made our way downstairs. We made our way to the end of the plane and down the stairs. I blinked, looking around me, making sure I was in the right place; we were amazed by the sight before us. The corporal and flight sergeant must have been busy last night. There in the hangar they had made an assault course. It spanned nearly the full length of the hangar.

Crates had been stacked strategically around the base, nets were pinned to the floor, ropes hung from the plane, tied to the wings.

Flight Sergeant Tanner cleared his throat. I expect you to complete this course each morning first thing. This course should take you no less than five minutes to complete!" he bellowed. "You will each be timed; I expect all of you to improve your times each day. If any of you fail to beat or match your time, you will repeat the course until you do. Have I made myself clear?"

"Yes," we grumbled in unison.

"It's 'Yes, Flight Sergeant'. I repeat, 'have I made myself clear?"

"Yes, Flight Sergeant!" We all braced up.

"Good. Now Corporal Jameson here will demonstrate the course in front of you. You will then line up at the start post in the order you are in now. I will tell each of you when to start the course."

The corporal lined himself up at the start. "Watch closely, I will only demonstrate this once."

We watched as the Corporal completed the course in front of us. It looked impossible. He ran to the first set of crates; there were three piled on top of each other. He climbed up to the top and jumped down. The drop must have been at least ten feet. He then jumped clean over three more crates, using his hands as a springboard. He got to the net and crawled under, using his powerful arms to propel himself forward. Eventually, he got to the rope hanging from the wing of the plane. He climbed up the rope with ease and pulled himself onto the plane. He ran across the wing and climbed over the plane to the wing at the other side of the plane. He ran across the wing to the second rope and climbed down. He ran towards us crossing the yellow and black tape, marking the end of the course.

His breathing was slightly more accelerated than normal, and his cheeks were slightly rosy, but he had not even broken a sweat. "Three minutes and fifty-eight seconds. An adequate time, Corporal" the flight sergeant declared. "Okay, cadet, you're up," he said, turning to Andy, who was first in line.

"In three, two, one... Go, go, go!" he screamed.

The boys were first in line Andy, Nick and Paul. After them, it was me and then Lacey. Last in the line-up was Duckface. She was clearly not impressed with having to take part.

Flight Sergeant Tanner gave ten seconds between each person. When it was my turn, I sprinted from the start ready to attempt the course. It soon became apparent that we were all struggling to complete the course. None of us were in great condition.

I absolutely detested exercise. If I ever needed to lose weight I much preferred to diet. There were always new weight loss diets coming out, from diet pills to meal-replacement shakes. Juice Plus was taking the world by storm. They consisted of three juices a day to replace meals. Even the largest and most robust of women out there were turning into slim and slender beauties. I hated exercise; I avoided it at all costs.

Now I was faced with a near impossible task to complete, which required speed, strength, balance and agility. The only thing I had was balance, which I got from the years I spent in heels. Even now I still had on my knee-high leather boots with a chunky heel, not the most appropriate footwear for the task ahead. Still, I gave it my best shot.

I climbed up the first crate, climbing up was the easy part, although once I got to the top my fear of heights kicked in. Corporal Jameson was screaming at me to jump. "Don't be a pussy, jump now! You're wasting time, the clock's ticking!" he was shouting. I took a deep breath and jumped. The soles of my feet burned with the impact as they touched the ground.

I carried on running – I made my way over the crates and under the net. The hard part was climbing up the rope. Paul was in front of me; he had made his way to the top of the rope and saw me struggling. He yelled for me to climb. I tried my hardest, but I just didn't have the body strength to do it, I got halfway up when Paul, seeing that I was still dangling in mid-air, turned back to help. He pulled the rope with me still attached until I got up onto the wing of the plane. Once I was up he turned to carry on the course. By this time Lacey had got to the bottom of the rope, like me she faced the same struggles.

I pulled at the rope as hard as I could, helping her up as Paul had done with me. As soon as she reached the top we ran together to the other side of the plane. We helped each other down the rope and ran past the finish line.

We were all exhausted. We looked back to the assault course and saw Duckface struggling, under the netting still. She looked like a fish out of water. She had made a pathetic attempt at the course. She flapped under the netting. She was clearly not used to having to strain herself.

Flight Sergeant Tanner had enough at this point. "All of you here now!" he roared.

We lined up again. None of us had come close to the Corporal Jameson's time. "Today's exercise was to determine your skills, your strengths and your weaknesses. We watched each of you, throughout the course."

He carried on. "The course wasn't just about strength. It was also about teamwork. You took it upon yourselves to help your fellow comrades, which was commendable. It did not go unnoticed."

Corporal Jameson spoke up. "What I did notice was that although you helped your friends in need, you made no attempt to help those you do not have such strong feelings for." He addressed Lacey and Duckface as he spoke.

"If you are to succeed in this course, you must all work together, and put your feelings towards each other aside. We will work with you all individually as well at teach you to work as part of a team."

After the long and drawn out lecture, we all scurried back into the plane for breakfast. We all went up to the plane expecting some kind of hot meal. Instead lying across the bar were six energy bars and six fruit and nut mix bags.

"What's this?" I asked when we got upstairs. Corporal Jameson answered. "This... is breakfast. Not only will you be training as cadets, but you will be eating like them as well."

"This is going to be so much fun," Duckface groaned sarcastically. "I said I don't want to be part of this, so why am I being made to get involved?" She grumbled.

"Lola, I am doing this for your own good. This training will help you all in the future. Should the base be compromised, attack is not always the best solution. You all need to be capable of outrunning your enemy. I understand you don't want to take part in the defence lessons; however that alone makes your fitness regime all the more important, don't you agree?"

She glanced at the rest of us and shook her head. "Well, if it comes to it I can run. I don't see the need to do it until I absolutely have to. I've tried it today and quite frankly, I'm not a fan. I'm not doing any of it. I'm going back to bed."

With that, she stormed off. Flight Sergeant Tanner tried to stop her. "If that's your choice, I have to respect that. But I strongly advise you rethink your decision. For your own sake." He added.

She carried on walking, without saying a word she left in a huff.

The next few days passed; we did the assault course on a daily basis, the more we got into it, the easier it became. I spent a few hours each day training with Corporal Jameson. He was very strict and forceful, but he knew my limits better than I did.

We had a tight training schedule. The press-ups and sit-ups were killing me. Not to mention the cardio – with weights, I might add.

"Come on, I know you can do this. Two more!" Corporal James said, pushing me as I struggled through the pain of my most recent set of sit-ups. His powerful hands kept my feet firmly planted on the ground.

"It's so painful," I moaned.

"I know, but just push through the pain. It'll be over soon," he reassured me.

I battled through my final sit-ups and collapsed down on the floor. "Please tell me we're done for the day," I begged.

"Not quite," the corporal replied. "We'll take five and pick it back up again after. After smiles and sat down beside me, handing me a bottle of water.

"You're going well so far. I never said it was going to be easy." He slapped my leg playfully, but my body was aching all over.

"Ouch," I complained. "It hurts everywhere!"

The corporal laughed. "You'll be fine. Toughen up."

I threw my water bottle at him. I had already emptied it; I just didn't have the strength to talk back.

"Assaulting a corporal now, are we?" Jameson joked. "It's a good job we're off duty or I'll have had another fifty press-ups out of you."

I liked this side of him. When the occasion called for it, he was a forceful and very respected corporal. In his downtime he was a kind, funny and incredibly charming guy.

I hobbled back to my feet. "Okay, break's over with. What have you got in store for me now?" I asked.

He raised an eyebrow and grinned back at me.

After day three, we had our first lesson in weaponry. Both NCOs led us through a trapdoor in the ceiling and onto the roof. After all the time spent in the hangar, I never noticed the trapdoor above us.

As we each looked around us, we were amazed at what we saw. The infected had taken over the airbase and were walking around beneath us. Men, women and children, of all different ages were wandering aimlessly around the base. Alerted to our presence they headed towards the hangar. My fear of heights began to kick in. There was no safety guard on top of the roof; it was just a straight drop down. I backed away from the edge.

Rifles were laid out in front of us. Flight Sergeant Tanner addressed us all. "As you can see, this is why we're training. Ever since the main base was compromised, the infected have had full reign of the airbase. It's time for this to stop, we need to take back control and help our fellow survivors. Now is a good of a time as any to start. In front of you, you will find a sharpshooter rifle with scope."

I picked up my gun and held the scope up to my line of vision. "What do you want us to do? Take them out?" I asked.

I have to admit, I was rather excited. I loved shooting. Granted I had never shot anything live before, but I thought I could handle it.

"That's precisely what we want you to do. Jameson will give you a demonstration and show each of you how to hold, fire and reload your weapons. Think of this as target practice." He turned and looked at me. "You already have the stance, I can see that in the way you hold the rifle. I expect this shouldn't pose a problem for you."

I wasn't going to let anyone down. The rifle I was holding wasn't too dissimilar to the guns I was used to shooting back on the farm. They were a lot bigger, but it still felt natural to me. As the corporal was showing my teammates the ropes, I held the rifle back up, scoping out my targets.

The closer I examined the infected, the harder the task ahead seemed to be. Once I got past the disease-ridden, rotting corpse appearance, they were still people. They had their own family, friends and even children. Would I be able to live with myself afterwards?

Sensing my inner turmoil, Corporal Jameson came to my side. "They're not people anymore, it's the virus using their bodies. At this stage putting a bullet through their head is their only salvation. If you ended up like that what would you prefer?"

He was right, and with that I pulled the trigger. I fired the first shot, and got my target dead on. It was a woman, in her early thirties. She was well dressed, very much the WAG type. The infection didn't do her any favours; her face was starting to rot, her hair was all over the place and remnants of blood stained her once bright blonde locks. She had a vicious, hungry expression; she snarled before the bullet pierced her skull. She dropped instantly. I looked back at her after I took the shot; she certainly looked more peaceful in death.

Once I took my first shot, everyone around me started shooting. Rounds could be heard left, right and centre, the noise was deafening. Some shots met their targets whilst others went off slightly, either hitting the tarmac, throwing up dust and debris, or other body parts of the infected. Still they kept coming. I took aim again, this time I didn't get my target. Instead, I blew an arm off my target, a former military man. He looked down at the space where his arm used to be and snarled up at me. He didn't seem overly concerned with his newly missing limb, he started to advance forward until I met my target with my second shot.

It didn't take long for all our targets to fall. Once they were all down, Flight Sergeant Tanner called a ceasefire. Looking around the carnage we had caused, it was horrific. Body parts filled the area around us; blood seeped out from all orifices of the undead corpses forming deep red puddles surrounding the base. The stench of death filled the air. It was repulsive.

"Well done. You managed to dispatch of the enemy, but your ammunition is now low. You need to be more precise; there's no room for error. Imagine that each bullet in your rifle is your last. We will resume tomorrow." Flight Sergeant Tanner advised.

"But we've taken them all out, what will we shoot tomorrow?" Lacey asked.

"This isn't the last we'll see of them. If that was the case we would have taken back the whole site single handedly by now. No matter how many we kill, they carry on coming. I've been watching them for weeks now. They don't eat each other, but they have no issue with consuming the fallen. I can guarantee that the bodies will not be here in the morning; The others will take them away."

"How come we didn't see any of them when we first came into the airbase? Where are they all if they are not out here?" Paul asked.

Corporal Jameson replied, "They don't always reveal themselves, they seem to like to hide in the shadows, they only come out when they think it's worth it, when there's something of interest to them. There's more to them that meets the eye. They are already starting to show signs of predatory behaviour."

This was getting even more disturbing; these things were a lot more complex than I had originally imagined. I thought they were just simple, mindless eating machines, but they seemed to be adapting to their environment. They were starting to hunt.

"So why didn't you shoot them when you saw them?" I asked.

"We did at first, but you learn a lot more about the enemy when it's alive, not when it's dead," the flight sergeant replied.

I thought back to our time cooped up in the apartment. I spent hours watching Walter the warden trudge around the cars, looking through the glass as if trying to regain a lost memory. Andy beat me to it.

"When we were stuck in the apartment, we made a log of what they were doing. We took it in turns to watch them, and wrote what we saw in a notebook," he piped up.

The flight sergeant's eyes lit up. "You did? I would be very interested in seeing that book. Do you still have it?"

"Yes I packed it before we left," I told him. "Maybe if we pulled our resources together we could find out a bit more about these things?" I asked.

Flight Sergeant Tanner agreed.

Later on that day, when the flight sergeant was alone, I approached him with the book. If the infected were, as I suspected, starting to evolve, I wanted answers.

"Sergeant, here's the book you asked for," I said. "I have some questions. I haven't been in close contact with these things, but I've had more experience with them than the rest of the group." I recounted my encounters in the factory and the apartment. I told him about the girl I saw in the road and of the old man who once lived downstairs. I also told him about the incident in the apartment with the infected banging on the walls.

The flight sergeant listened intently to everything I told him. His face looked very puzzled.

"The fact that they made noise but made no attempt to get in, shows they are indeed using parts of the brain. To me it shows they are a lot more tactical than I imagined. They are also capable of working together which confirms my suspicions that they are indeed showing a predatory, pack mentality."

"Well, it still makes no sense, why did they make no attempt to get in?" I asked intrigued.

"All I can do is hazard a guess. On some level, they must have known they couldn't get in. Therefore, they made a noise to scare you and flush you out. Since they couldn't get to you, any attempt would be futile. They wanted you to go to them."

A shiver went down my spine. How could it be that a well-known virus could not only wipe out most of humanity, but also show signs of intelligence? I would never have believed that any of this was possible, let alone going on all around us.

"Given this new information, I must insist we reach the other hangars. You all have much more training to do, but from what I've learned so far, we cannot waste any time. Tonight we will prepare the vehicles, first thing tomorrow we are going to visit Hangar 5."

"What's Hangar 5?" I asked.

"Come with me." The Flight Sergeant whispered.

He took me back up to the roof. From the rooftop, we could see the whole base. The flight sergeant pointed to Hangar 5. It was the closest building to us. It was around half the size of the hangar we were currently in; it looked completely secure.

"What's in there?" I asked.

"Hangar 5 is our communications base. It also stores some of our military vehicles, as well as extra supplies.

"I will take a small team with me tomorrow; I want you and Lacey to stay here, you will be our eyes from above. If you see any of the infected, I want you to shoot them down. Do not aim too close to any of the vehicles, we will take any close by out at ground level, do you understand?"

"Yes, that's fine," I replied. It was very exciting – our first mission.

We went into the hangar and gathered everyone together. The flight sergeant ran through the plan and asked Nick, Andy and Paul to join him and Corporal Jameson.

"No, I'm sorry, Andy, you're not going," Duckface spat. Let's just say she wasn't overly thrilled with our decision to venture outside.

"Sergeant, I will not have my husband put himself in danger for something I don't even agree with."

"What exactly is it that you don't you agree with?" I asked her, slightly miffed.

It wasn't just her husband that was going out; it was also Lacey's husband and my fiancé. I didn't like the idea that they were going to be in danger any more than she did, but neither me nor Lacey stopped them or made a big deal about it. They were old enough to make their own decisions.

"We don't need to go anywhere, we're safe here. Who's to say anyone's even alive in there?" she replied. "I'm sorry I've said no, and that's final. Andy, you're staying with me."

"I'm sure Andy can speak for himself," the corporal replied, trying to diffuse the situation. "We are not forcing anyone to do anything they don't want to do."

"Andy, mate, what do you want to do?" Nick asked.

All eyes were now on Andy. He looked uncomfortable as he shifted around, clearly not quite sure what to do or say. I could tell that he was trying to avoid confrontation, the atmosphere was starting to feel very awkward.

"I'm sorry, Lola, but I'm going. I know you're worried, but it's okay. We'll all be armed, and I'm not alone. I'll come straight back to you, I promise." He tried to put his arm around her but she was having none of it.

"Whatever. Do what you want then. Go out and get eaten, and then when you get infected you can find a nice infected girlfriend and then you'll be happy," she said. With that, she stormed off again. Her tantrums were starting to become a daily occurrence. She hated not being in control.

"What was all that about?" Nick asked, shaking his head.

"I have no idea, but fuck it, can't be arsed with it." Andy shrugged.

"Glad to have you on board," the corporal said patting him firmly on the back.

That was the first time I had ever seen Andy stick up for himself. I kept it to myself, but I was so proud of him. It was a step in the right direction. Duckface seriously needed to learn that she couldn't control everyone. She was acting like a spoilt child.

She stayed upstairs sulking the whole of that night. Everyone seemed a little on edge. It was as if we were preparing for battle. We tried to keep conversation light-hearted, but we all knew tomorrow our boys were leaving the safety and security of our hangar. It was really our first mission.

Chapter 8

Hangar 5

The next morning we all did our regular lap around the assault course. Afterwards, Corporal Jameson took us into the ammunition store. He picked us each rifles, the ones we had used to practice with, as well as a handgun and two boxes of ammunition. He told us to keep the handguns on us at all times should the worst happen.

Lacey and I took these to the roof and set ourselves up. We each took a corner. We agreed between ourselves which areas we would cover. Lacey covered the left side whilst I stayed to the right.

The infected were nowhere to be seen. The trail of blood, guts and body parts could still be seen staining the ground beneath us, but just as the flight sergeant had said, the bodies had vanished.

On closer inspection, I could see that trails of blood where the bodies had evidently been dragged. The trails led to the other side of the base away from Hangar 5. This was a good sign, it meant the infected weren't hiding out where the boys were going.

We heard the automatic shutters open up beneath us, the boys were making their way out. As soon as the car was in view, I followed the area around them with my scope, my finger poised on the trigger, in case the infected came too close.

Flight Sergeant Tanner had told us to aim for the head, but if there were too many to also aim for the legs, as apparently would slow them down.

They managed to make their way over to Hangar 5 with no problems or unwanted guests. The infected were nowhere to be seen.

As soon as they got to their destination, the flight sergeant stepped out and punched in the code for the building. I aimed my scope into the building and saw all the boys had their guns at the ready. I felt a lot safer knowing that we were all well-armed.

As the shutters came up on the hangar in front of us, I could see the lights flicker on. I saw three figures in the entrance come running towards the boys. I held my gun up ready to fire when I saw the boys lower their weapons.

All three figures were dressed in combat uniforms. They were all still alive. They all greeted the flight sergeant by snapping to attention and greeted the boys with friendly handshakes. They seemed to be talking among themselves and introducing one another. I aimed my scope towards them, straining to get a closer look.

I was brought back to reality when I heard a loud bang ring out from Lacey's rifle. I quickly checked my scope again to see if the boys were okay, thinking she had shot one of the men we had seen come out the building. Everyone was okay, but they were all looking to the left. They all ran inside ushered by the new faces, whilst Flight Sergeant Tanner pressed the release button on the shutters, lowering it down. I had no idea what was going on.

I looked to my left and saw crowds of the infected running out from behind the hangar in front of us, making their way to the shutters. They were running at full speed towards the entrance. I had never seen the infected run before. They looked a lot less human – more like animals. Their disease-ridden faces snarled and bit the air as they advanced towards their targets.

My heart fell. I knew if they got to the boys that would be it. Lacey and I sped into action. They were starting to pour out from both sides of the building. I immediately took the first two down. Still they kept coming; there must have been about thirty of them. It didn't take long for Lacey and me to dispose of them all, but it was a lot harder to hit a running target. We had used up all our ammunition. It was time to reload.

The speed of these creatures frightened me. In all my previous encounters they had been slow and shuffling. I was completely baffled as to why they were suddenly capable of running at such speeds.

After we were sure they were all down, and definitely weren't getting back up, we did a sweep of the area around us.

Had we not been on the roof, the boys wouldn't have been so lucky.

My heart was pounding; adrenaline was running through me, I was so relieved the boys had made it inside, but I felt so helpless from the roof. If anything was inside there was nothing either Lacey or me could do about it. They were out of our sights.

I looked down to the fresh corpses now lying on the ground. The infected must have been lying in wait; the sound of the shutter going up had clearly alerted them and prompted them to attack. They were clearly getting a lot more advanced, since my last encounter.

We sat on the roof watching and waiting for the boys to return. After an hour, we still saw no sign of them. I was starting to get worried. Still we checked the areas in front and around us, trying to avoid any nasty surprises, above all else we had to make sure their return journey was safe.

Another half hour passed. We heard the trapdoor spring back; Duckface had come up to join us. She had never been out here before. She looked incredibly pale against the sunlight. She hadn't seen any natural light in over a week.

She made her way over to me, and gasped when she saw the dead bodies in front of her. I doubt she had ever seen a dead body before, never mind a rotting, bloody disintegrated corpse like the ones laid out before us. Lacey and I were starting to become immune to the haunting sights.

After sitting outside for so long you tend to get used to them, the bodies were starting to blend in with the surroundings, even the stench didn't bother us anymore.

Duckface just didn't seem to understand this new world or grasp how dangerous the infected creature were. All she had seen of the infected was what she saw peering out the window at the flat. She was completely closed off from the world.

She sat next to me clearly shaken up. "What's happened?" she asked.

"The infected started running out from around the back of the buildings, just as the boys were going inside. Lacey spotted them first and fired the first shot; I started shooting just after, we managed to get them all before they got in," I replied.

"Is everyone okay?" she asked.

"Yes they all made it in okay – not seen them since and that was an hour and a half ago."

Lacey looked over to me and raised her eyebrow. She stayed in her position scoping out the area.

"Look at all those bodies, did you kill all of them?" she asked. There was no sign of sarcasm or judgement in her voice; she was genuinely intrigued.

"All the ones on this side," I said, pointing to the area in front of us. "Lacey took out the ones on the other side."

She nodded. She didn't say anything else; she simply stared at the carnage in front of us.

I heard the sound of a gunshot off in the distance. It sounded like it came from inside the building, but I couldn't be sure. We stayed silent as I went back to checking the area. I wasn't taking any chances if I saw any of the infected; I was taking them out.

Twenty minutes later we heard the shutters opening; Corporal Jameson was the first out. He ran over to the car he had abandoned when they first entered the hangar and turned it around. Luckily they had opted to use Andy's car.

I looked back towards the opening of the hangar and saw two four-by-fours slowly driving out. The boys were still armed, and all looked a little tired and out of breath, but apart from that they seemed okay. They were also joined by the new faces.

The short journey back to the hangar was a lot less eventful than the first. Lacey and I were still on our guard, although thankfully we didn't need to use our rifles again.

As soon they had got back inside, we left our posts and made our way back into the hangar. As I was about to make my way down, I glanced up at Hangar 5. The infected were starting to reappear again, I quickly held my rifle back up, to get a closer look through the scope. They weren't running this time; they looked more quizzical. They made their way over to the newly decapitated bodies and started to drag them around towards the back of the building. There were a lot more of them this time, at least thirty had slithered out from the shadows. A chill ran down my spine, I chose to ignore them and made my way downstairs, eager to greet the boys and our new friends.

*

The following events are recounts from Nick and Paul, who filled me in, shortly after returning from Hanger 5.

After we had made our way to the roof, they were taken to the ammunition store. They were also given handguns, as well as a bigger assault rifle. They were given instructions on how to use both, and they were also given bayonets in case hand-to-hand combat was necessary. This was something that the flight sergeant and the corporal were yet to cover with the rest of us.

They got into the back of the car with Andy, whilst the corporal took the wheel. They were all surprised as they got out into the open as to how the area around the hangar was so clear. It was as if the zombie apocalypse was a mere figment of their imagination, or more likely – the undeads day off.

As soon as they reached their destination, Flight Sergeant Tanner ordered them to stay put and to keep their weapons at the ready and most importantly, be prepared. As soon as he punched the code into the door the shutters sprang to life. They both admitted they weren't paying attention to what was going on around them; they were trying to get a good look into the hangar. They said that the entrance had two army trucks parked in front of the door, but they could see three men running towards them, armed and in combat gear. As soon as they saw the flight sergeant came to attention. They looked at Nick, Andy and Paul quizzically and, getting a nod of approval from the flight sergeant, they went over to introduce.

The first soldier was a guy called Josh. He was in his mid-twenties, but he looked a lot younger. He had a boyish face; he didn't seem capable of growing any facial hair, his hair was cut short, he was very light blond. He had blue eyes and a rather skinny build.

The second soldier to introduce himself was a man named Greg, he was a fair few years older than Josh, in his mid-forties. He was a lot more filled out than Josh. The beginnings of a beer belly had started to peer through. He looked a lot more rugged and manly than Josh did. His hair was starting to grey at the sides, and his greying stubble showed he certainly hadn't had access to a razor for some time.

The third soldier was a tall, broad, handsome man. He was well over six foot, in his late twenties with an olive skin tone and dark hair, he was called Leon. He looked a lot more the army type than the other two did. He had a stern face at first but smiled and greeted the boys charmingly.

"We've got company!" sang out Corporal Jameson. Yet, even as the group swung round to see so many loping figures making straight for them, the echo of Lacey's incoming round dropped the three newcomers straight into firing positions.

"*Incoming!*" called one.

"Friendly fire, friendly fire!" snapped Flight Sergeant Tanner, raising a first.

"Whose?" demanded the other, eyes still questing for the source of the shot.

"Our guardian angels," Tanner said with a smile. "Explain later, just get that bloody door down!"

It was then; when they heard Lacey's shot being fired they all stepped back following the line of fire. From the corners of the building, they saw the infected running out towards them. It took them all off guard.

"Quick, get in the building, leave the car," Leon shouted, motioning the boys inside.

"I'll get the door, all of you in. Corporal, take flank," the flight sergeant barked.

As soon as the group were inside they saw the infected dropping all around them. They took a step back from the door not wanting to be caught up in the crossfire whilst Lacey and I took the remaindered of the undead out.

Once the doors were closed, and they were safely inside the Sergeant smiled. "Those girls did good."

"Girls?" Josh asked "Sir, they did that?"

Corporal Jameson nodded. "Yes, we didn't want to put them in danger, so I set them up on the roof and left them with orders, which they executed perfectly." The pride in Corporal Jameson's voice did not go a miss.

The sergeant agreed. "We have much to discuss. Is it just the three of you here?"

Leon stepped forward. "No, sir. Professor Hyatt is with us as well."

"Good, please take me to him," he addressed Leon as he ushered him further into the building.

Corporal Jameson stayed with the boys and the rest of the soldiers. "Okay, men, the plan is we take what we can carry and we make our way back over to our hangar. Is the area secure?" he asked the soldiers.

Josh and Greg looked at each other "Yes, sir," they replied in unison.

As Nick and Paul took in their new surroundings, they saw the four-by-fours in a better light. One was a green pick-up truck with an oversized Mercedes badge on the front. The pickup was covered with a canvas tent high off the ground.

The corporal pointed to the truck. "Let's start filling this truck, gather all the supplies you can. I want you all working together on this one. I will head to the communications base and pack the equipment ready for transport."

"But, sir, the communications are down, we've been trying to use it ever since we got ourselves trapped in here. We didn't think anyone was alive out there," Josh told him.

"Stand down. We will take it all over to the other building, and set up there." The Corporal ordered.

Josh nodded. Nick and Paul followed them over to the supply area. The soldiers took them to a small warehouse. It was filled with small beds, rucksacks, uniforms and MREs. It was like walking into an army camp shop; it was full.

The boys started carrying the beds and rucksacks to the truck. Uniforms, bulletproof vests, camping equipment, clothes and footwear were next.

"I'm sure the girls will love their new shoes," Paul joked.

"So what are these girls like?" Josh asked, a little too eager.

"Taken," Nick replied defensively.

Andy explained. "My wife, Lola, doesn't get involved with the rest of us, she doesn't agree with what we're doing, she's a big fan of gun control. She just stays on the plane. She doesn't get out much." He sighed.

"Sounds to me she needs a wake-up call, the rules of the world have changed," Greg chimed in as he passed. "No offence, mate."

"Ha! She's needs to get her head out her arse more like," Paul sniggered. "No offence," he added quickly.

"What about the rest, how many of you are they?"

"There's only two others, the ones on the roof shooting the shit out of those things earlier," Nick added, "my fiancé and his wife," he said, pointing to Paul.

"They're a lot more grounded, although they don't really get on with Lola," Nick continued.

"I have no idea why," Paul put in sarcastically. "What's life without a bit of girl's drama?"

"Okay, that's enough. Look, I'm sorry she's acting like this, but there's nothing I can do about it. She is the way she is," Andy huffed, trying to defend her.

"We're not having a go at you, mate," Nick started. "It's just –"

Andy interrupted. "Don't worry, forget it. George is over there with us as well, you know the old guy that runs this place?" Andy tried to change the subject.

"Oh yeah, I've seen him a few times. Never thought the old sod would make it if I'm honest," Greg said, happy to change the conversation.

They carried on emptying the room until the truck was full. "No point in taking the MREs, I already know your camp's full of them," Josh told Nick.

By the time the corporal had come back with the communications equipment the boys were just about done.

"I think we're done here, let's go and find the flight sergeant," the corporal suggested. Before anyone could utter another word, they heard a gunshot fire towards the back end of the building. The shot came from inside.

Corporal Jameson and the airmen grabbed their handguns and ran to the area where Flight Sergeant Tanner and Leon had disappeared off to. The boys followed their lead and ran after them.

They ran through a clean, clinical room – a makeshift science lab. As they turned the corner to the room where the flight sergeant and Leon were they all stopped. There in front of them was a padded room. Two glass windows overlooked the room where the boys had stopped. As they peered through the windows, they saw an infected solider lying dead on the floor, a bullet through his skull. The flight sergeant stood over the body, blood splattered down his shirt, whilst Leon and the professor stood behind him.

They boys had no idea what had happened but speculated that one of the soldiers must have got infected, so had been locked in the room, either before or after they died.

Flight Sergeant Tanner walked out of the room, cleaning the end of his handgun. "Have any of you come into contact with Private Tembury?" he asked, the soldiers shook their heads. "Have any of you been bitten?" he carried on forcefully. Again they shook their heads. "Good, I think it's about time we headed back, don't you?" he asked the corporal.

"Yes, flight sergeant," the Corporal replied.

They walked back to the cars in silence. Leon climbed in the driver's side of the truck whilst the flight sergeant and the rest of the boys climbed in the second four-by-four.

Corporal Jameson opened the shutters and turned Andy's car around, heading back to base. The flight sergeant headed out first, with the boys and the communication equipment. Leon was the last to leave, closing the shutters and securing the building on his way out before hopping into the car with the corporal.

Chapter 9

Theoretical Science

As soon as I had climbed down from the roof everyone was already buzzing around. The boys were busy unloading the truck by the time me and Lacey made our way over to them.

As soon as Nick saw me he put the supplies down and came running over to me, he pulled me into his arms and kissed me.

"Hi, baby," I said, smiling. "Did you miss me?"

He laughed. "Yes I did. You did well up there, I'm really proud of you."

"Told you I had a good shot!" I retorted as he loosened his grip around me.

Flight Sergeant Tanner came over to us. "Girls, I'm impressed with your work today. You got us all out of a tight spot; I'm very grateful."

"As are we." Leon came forward and offered his hand. "We haven't been introduced yet; I'm Leon, and this is Josh and

Greg," he said pointing to the two others. They both turned around to us and waved but carried on unloading.

"Your corporal tells me you've been training. You're in good hands; Corporal Jameson trained me when I started. You'll be Rock Apes in no time."

"Rock Apes?" I asked puzzled. I had never heard the terminology before. Was this a good thing or bad?

"It's just a nickname we use sometimes." Leon explained.

"I don't get it." Lacey replied, she was equally perplexed.

"I'm sure if you ask George, the old boy will tell you what it means and how it came about." Leon finished.

"We brought you back some presents," Paul interrupted. He was grinning from ear to ear.

Lacey and I looked at each other; our faces beamed. We liked the word PRESENTS very much.

Paul and Nick turned around, holding two combat uniforms. They each had a pair of boots in their hands, too.

"Your size I believe, madam," said Nick, offering me the shoes.

"I don't like these presents," I replied pouting.

"Me neither," said Lacey with the same disappointed expression.

"Well, if you're going to act the part you need to look it," Paul laughed. He defended his manhood anticipating a swift kick. Lacey did not look impressed.

Corporal Jameson took pity on us. "These trousers may be a bit too big," he said, handing us each a sewing box. "Feel free to alter them if it makes you feel better. You can take them in at the sides, so they don't fall or get too baggy?"

"Thanks, I'm sure we'll find a way to alter these, won't we, Lacey?" I said looking at her, grinning mischievously, a new idea starting to form in my head.

With our new clothes in hand, we headed up to the plane.

"What are we going to do with these? I can't even sew," she asked as we threw the clothes down on the sofa.

"I have no idea, but I'm not wearing them as they are. Have you felt how heavy they are?" I complained.

We tried them on to see how bad they actually were. We looked at each other and burst out laughing.

"Oh God, we look like a bunch of idiots, it's so baggy I can hardly walk," Lacey laughed.

"Marshmallow comes to mind. We need to do something about this," I grinned. "I don't care where we are I'm not having people see me like this."

As Duckface walked in, we both fell silent, our laughter quickly subsiding. Duckface was getting particularly hard to read these days. One minute she was fine, the next she would be in a stinking mood. We never knew what would come next with her. We looked at her, slightly apprehensive. This girl took PMS to a whole new level.

She turned to me. "I don't want us to fall out. I know I haven't been getting involved, I can't do what either of you do. You really helped them today; Andy might not be alive if it wasn't for you. Who knows what would have happened." She seemed sincere enough.

I appreciated her coming forward, but it wasn't that easy to forgive her behaviour. "I'm not being funny, but that's why we agreed to the training. You wonder why everyone's off with you, it's the same old Lola we're all used to. You don't seem to care about anyone else apart from yourself."

"Okay, I'm not going to argue. At least let me help you with these uniforms. I can sew; I'll help you make them a little more appealing. What do you think?"

I looked at Lacey. She didn't look overly impressed, but we both knew we needed someone who knew how to sew, and unless George was a veteran and part-time crochet artist, we knew she was the best we could get, given the circumstances.

"Yeah fine, you can help us with the uniforms. But don't think that it makes up for all the shitty stuff you've said and done," Lacey replied, pulling off her new ensemble.

"That's fine, thanks," Duckface mumbled. She wasn't happy with Lacey's response, she expected us to go running into her arms overjoyed by her revelation, playing best buddies again. As nice as that thought was, life just didn't work that way.

Rome wasn't built in a day. It was a good start, though.

We spent the next couple of hours ripping, cutting and sewing up our uniforms. By the time we had finished, there was more material on the floor, than there was on the finished product.

I had decided to keep my leather boots. They had a bit of a heel, but were chunky enough still to be considered sensible, to us anyway. In order to keep my boots, I had to reinvent my military trousers into hot pants. Running around the hangar training had us all sweating. We didn't have the luxury of air conditioning so I figured I should stay light. I kept the pockets as they were for storage, but the rest of the material had to go.

The shirt didn't need as much work. I undid a few of the buttons and tied it into a knot above my waist. I rolled my sleeves up to my elbows and pulled the shirt in at the sides.

Using a piece of discarded material from the trousers, I made myself a headband, giving the whole outfit a Rambo effect.

Lacey followed my lead and did the same. Once we were both happy we had shredded enough unnecessary weight, we went back to the hangar to see if the boys needed help.

As soon as they saw us step out from the plane they all turned to face us. The Sergeant looked at us as if to say 'What the hell have you done to my uniforms'. The corporal couldn't help but laugh.

We looked towards our partners. Nick and Paul were both in hysterics, as Lacey and I looked at each other puzzled.

"What?" we asked simultaneously.

"Only you two could turn an official military uniform into a fancy dress outfit," Paul said with a laugh.

"It looks like you're on your way to a hen do," Nick chuckled.

"Well, I've certainly never seen that before," the corporal smiled. "As long as you're happy with them."

"I trust it won't impede in your training?" Flight Sergeant Tanner asked, seeing the funny side of it too.

I had the perfect response already lined up. "Au contraire! The boots were too heavy, so I decided to stick with my leather boots. I kept the pockets in my shorts, extra space for more ammunition. As you can see the whole outfit is a lot lighter than it originally was, meaning we will keep our speed up and not have any unnecessary weight pulling us down."

Corporal Jameson grinned. "You make a fair argument. I think you both look lovely," he said, trying to keep the peace.

I noticed the Professor over in the corner, unpacking his equipment. I went over to introduce myself.

"Hi, Professor." I smiled as I shook his hand.

"Hello, my dear," he replied, caught a bit off guard with my new outfit. "I do hope the flight sergeant didn't fool you into thinking that attire was official military standard," He laughed. He had a well-spoken English accent, rather posh. He pronounced every word perfectly, making clear that he was extremely well educated. As soon as I heard his voice I was reminded of Stephen Fry, he sounded exactly like him.

He was a typical English gentleman. He was in his early sixties; he spent his younger years at Cambridge University, where he studied the natural sciences along with chemical engineering. After graduating from Cambridge with honours, he started out his career as a lab assistant on the Cambridge Biomedical Campus. After a great number of years in Cambridge, he moved to Cheshire to take up a new position with AstraZeneca, based in Alderley Edge.

When the RAF established a base on the airfield, AstraZeneca sent over a team of scientists to assist and gather research needed for their project. Professor Hyatt led the team in question.

"No, I wasn't fond of the uniform he issued us with, so I made some minor adjustments," I joked.

"How very resourceful of you," he replied with a smile. He was a kind man and I soon learned he had a quirky sense of humour.

"Our flight sergeant explained that you have been researching the virus?" I asked him, changing the subject and getting back to the original reason I approached him.

"Yes, I came to the base in order to find out first-hand the way the virus was spreading from human to human. My seniors would not allow an infected person to enter the laboratory, so instead they agreed I could bring a team here, to conduct my research."

"So where is the rest of your team?" I asked. I already knew the answer – if they weren't here the chances are they were dead, or worse infected.

"They were in the main base, where our main laboratory was. They were still inside when the lockdown took place." He sighed. "Not only did I lose my team, I also lost all of my research along with it."

"I'm so sorry, Professor." I said as I saw the pain in his eyes. "I take it you were working on a cure?"

"Yes, that was the intention. However, the more we studied the Ebola virus, the more complex it became. It started to evolve as it spread its way through the continents. My research is inconclusive at this stage, I'm very sorry to say."

"How do you mean it evolved?" I asked.

He pulled over two crates and offered me a seat.

As he sat down opposite me, he explained. "Well, the Ebola virus on average has a timeframe of around twenty-one days from infection to death. This new strain of virus takes at best seventy-two hours. As the virus passed from human to human, the population of the infected accelerated dramatically. What we don't know as of yet is how the virus is able to reanimate the deceased and at what point in the viral timeline it started to mutate."

This was starting to go over my head, but I tried to take in as much as possible.

He carried on. "Viruses such as Ebola are very resistant. They adapt to their surroundings. They only have one need, to stay alive. In order to stay alive, they need to infect a host, they feed off the host's nutrients until there is nothing left. Once there is nothing left they must find another, and repeat the process, so on and so forth."

I tried to take all this new information in. I knew very little about the virus, but I was eager to learn more.

"So does this explain why the infected are turning into zombies?" It felt strange using the word zombie. Zombies are what you see in horror films; they were not part of our everyday life. Or at least they never used to be.

"In a way, yes. I have a theory on why the corpses are reanimating themselves, but I have yet to discover the research to back it up," he explained.

"My theory is that the virus has mutated itself in such a way that it can take over parts of the brain, and keep it functioning for extended periods of time. In science terms, it has been able to access and work alongside the cerebral cortex. As a computer would, it has rebooted certain sections of the brain to enable movement and other primary senses."

I started to understand vaguely at best. "So it kept the brain working, so it had more time to find someone else to infect?" I asked.

"Precisely. As soon as the virus hits the reanimation stage, it has exhausted nearly all the nutrients from the host. It becomes desperate to find a new host, to survive. Along the way, the virus must have worked out; it could stay in the host's body by ingesting the nutrients of another host, whilst passing the on the virus to said host, completing the chain."

It all made perfect sense. The virus, like us, was just trying to survive. It explained why the only way to kill the infected was to shoot them in the head. I still had more questions.

"This would explain the new behaviour the infected are showing," I told him.

He didn't seem to understand. I explained to him my involvement with the infected and what myself and the flight sergeant observed of them.

He sat listening closely to everything I had to say. "That's very interesting. The sergeant mentioned the predatory behaviour showing amongst the infected. Again I have a few theories as to why this could be happening. But lack the concrete evidence."

He went on to explain the various functions of the brain. He explained that within the cerebral cortex, there were lobes, which control human functions. The Professor thought that the virus could only access certain brain functions; however, he believes that the longer the virus is present in the body and is able to sustain itself, the more power it had to reboot the lobes and access more of the brain. He compared this to a child growing into an adult. He believed that the virus started its life when it entered the human body. As the virus aged, he believed it learned to understand the body of the host, and manipulate the functions in order to increase its life expectancy.

This explained why the infected had started out as stumbling slow movers. After surviving for an extended period, and by feeding, they must have gained the energy and the intelligence to restart other areas of the brain. Giving them enhanced features to what they originally had...

"Does the Flight Sergeant Tanner know about this?" I asked.

"Not until today," the Professor replied. "I suggest you speak directly with the flight sergeant on how he wishes to proceed." He quickly changed the subject. "Please excuse me. I am going to reacquaint myself with an old friend." He got up and walked over to the other side of the hangar, where George was sitting, perched nicely on a fold-up camp chair. He left me alone to take in the new information.

I sat there for a while, processing. I felt nothing. I didn't know what to think, things seemed to be getting worse and it was out of all of our control. I hated not knowing what was coming next. In normal life I was always extremely organised, Nick was always happy to go with the flow, I always needed to know what I was doing from one day to the next. Don't get me wrong, I didn't think way into the future, but I couldn't get in the car and drive without having a destination in mind.

At that moment, I felt like I was driving around a dark countryside trying to find my destination, but I couldn't see past my own headlights. I was completely lost.

The advanced behaviour the infected had begun to show chilled me to the bone. The infected already terrified me. I just couldn't comprehend this new threat. What hopes did we have of survival if these things could communicate? What if they were able to carry out a strategic attack? There were too many unknowns for my liking.

I knew I needed to speak to Flight Sergeant Tanner about this; he would know what to do. I tried to put it to the back of my mind for the time being, we had more new faces around, I was sure the dynamics of the group would change yet again.

I made my way over to the rest of the group. They had unpacked the entire contents of the truck, and the boys were keen to play with all the camping gadgets they had found.

I headed over to the Flight Sergeant Tanner, keen to get his views on the recent information I had just learnt.

Over the past week and a half of knowing Flight Sergeant Tanner, he never failed to look out for me. He was a figure of authority, yet he cared for me as a father would for a daughter. He had told us he had three daughters; all were in their early twenties. Unfortunately, they had been locked in the building when he gave the orders to shut it down. I knew this weighed heavy on his heart. I couldn't begin to understand the pain he was in. He knew at that point they were gone.

"Flight Sergeant, what are we going to do about all this?" I said, my head still completely baffled

"Don't say anything just yet. We will hold a meeting later on today once everyone's settled in, and we'll work this out together," he replied gently. He was very reassuring.

I wandered off, still collecting my thoughts. Now that the adrenaline had worn off, my shoulder was starting to ache from the kickback of the rifle. I stood there rolling my shoulder around trying to soothe the ache.

Nick strolled up to me and grabbed me from behind.

"Does someone need a massage?" he asked, rubbing my shoulder.

I turned to face him. "Please," I smiled. He didn't give the best massages in the world. He often got bored halfway through, but something was better than nothing, plus it would take my mind away from the crowd of the infected, waiting patiently for the right moment to catch us off guard and devour us whole.

Chapter 10

Mending Fences

Flight Sergeant Tanner called a meeting later that night. I was about ready for bed when he called us all together. We all went through to the dining room upstairs, on board the plane. We all just about fitted around the large table. The flight sergeant stayed stood up.

"I trust you have all introduced yourselves to one another?" he asked, breaking the ice.

We all nodded. "Good, now let's carry on with the main reason I've called you all here." He was a straight down to business kind of guy.

He proceeded to tell us about the Professor's findings and a brief background on the events since the virus took over.

The Professor explained to us all what his current theories were in terms of the way the virus evolved. We all sat in silence as we listened carefully.

After he was done, Flight Sergeant Tanner addressed us all again. "Now, the question is, what do you want to do about it?"

We all looked at him confused. I didn't have a clue where he was going with this.

"I want to take back the base. We have been trapped in here too long. I refuse to sit here withering away whilst the enemy takes control," he said, pointing outside. "We should be out there searching for civilians and helping those in need. This is one war I refuse to lose."

"Okay, flight sergeant, what's the plan?" Leon asked, clearly in agreement.

"Simple, we clean this base up. If you see anyone infected, you shoot to kill. Any survivors you bring back to me."

From that point on, we all had a part to play. Flight Sergeant Tanner didn't want me or Lacey to go out, so he put us back on the roof as snipers. I was happy with that, I much preferred shooting from long range. I was still dying to get my hands on the .50 cal in the ammunition store. It looked complicated, but I was dying to try it out.

Although Duckface still refused to take part in any exercises she reluctantly agreed to look after any new survivors we came across, as a welcoming committee. I already felt sorry for the new survivors who would have to deal with her. If she didn't like someone she was often rude and abrupt, you really had to know how to take her.

In the meantime she agreed to help the Professor, alongside George, carry on the research. She fit right in. All she ever was before all this was an office bitch. The role suited her down to the ground.

I was glad she was still keeping her distance, although we were in a much bigger area than we were at the apartment; it didn't make her any less annoying.

Hers and Andy's relationship didn't seem to be doing so well. Andy seemed to be spending more time with the boys, and seemed reluctant to stay by her side, where she wanted him. The odd time I saw them together neither of them seemed happy, poor Andy looked miserable. I caught her a few times shamelessly flirting with Josh and Leon. They were always polite to her, but I could tell in the way they looked at one another they thought she had a screw lose.

She reverted back to her old ways. Now that there were new people around, she wanted to play up to every single one of them, boasting about herself. Even her mannerisms were over-exaggerated. It was like watching a child hyped up on sugar let loose around a sweet shop.

I couldn't help but cringe. She asked pointless questions, and when people responded to her, she would pretend to listen and pout her lips (ERGO the duckface) as she nodded, with the occasional 'yep' as if in agreement with the other person.

It was like watching the Churchill dog the way her head was bobbing up and down. I'd happily watch that advert constantly on repeat than listen to her whining high-pitched voice.

The flight sergeant split the boys into two teams. He led the first team, which consisted of Nick, Paul and Greg, while

Corporal Jameson led the second team alongside Leon, Andy and Josh.

They had all started training together within their teams, the airmen showed the boys how to use the weapons, and they started their lessons in close combat.

Lacey and I spent our training up on the roof. I figured we might as well practice on the real thing. I preferred it on the roof. With Duckface being in such close proximity of me and a gun, the urge to shoot was far too tempting. At least on the roof both Lacey and I could get away from her.

Flight Sergeant Tanner trained all the boys for the first phase of his plan. Hangar 5 contained spare fencing and barbed wire; he wanted to build a fence between our hangar and Hangar 5 so we could easily move between buildings without threat from the infected. In order to do this, he needed us all to work together. Lacey and I were to protect them from above; both teams would pick up the fencing and the wire. One team would build whilst the others stood guard.

Even George got involved with this plan; he volunteered to be an extra set of eyes on top of the roof of Hangar 5. Armed with a rifle he left with the rest.

I wasn't overly keen on the boys being out in the open, but I felt better knowing at least I could protect them from above.

As the trucks made their way to the hangar, the infected were nowhere to be seen. Although I couldn't see them, I knew they were around. I wasn't taking any prisoners, as soon as I saw one I'd take them out. We had plenty of ammo, and we knew the other buildings were full of weapons too. We had more than enough.

It wasn't long before the boys reappeared, with a truck full of fencing. The hangers were at least eight hundred yards apart. It would take the boys a few full days to secure the area. Like clockwork they started to erect the fencing, the distance between the fences was the size of a small road, it encompassed both shutters on either side, out of arm's reach. Barbed wire was to be positioned at the top and bottom of each fence.

Hopefully, this would keep the infected out. It wasn't long before we spotted our first kill of the day. This one was a slow mover. It looked slightly worse for wear; its left arm was missing, and part of its jaw had been ripped clean off. It was not a pretty sight. He wasn't getting anywhere quickly in that state; I saw the hunger in his eyes as it shuffled towards the boys. A split second after I saw him, I blew his head clean off. Chunks of flesh scattered the area around him as his body slumped to the floor.

I wasn't taking any chances. My aim was beginning to show improvement.

Jameson had advised me to aim ahead of my target to help whilst they were on the move. It was taking some getting used to, but I wasn't wasting as many bullets. I took it as a good sign.

The boys looked around upon hearing the sound of my rifle. Corporal Jameson shouted at them to get back to work, they couldn't afford to lose focus.

They carried on as Lacey and I took out three more. They seemed to be coming all around us – we stayed vigilant. I heard four shots fired from the building opposite; George must have spotted a few. We would be okay as long as hordes of them didn't come running. The boys finished working as the sun went down.

By the end of the first day I had managed to shoot fifteen, Lacey got thirteen and George took out eighteen. George took the lead. On his way back to base he stopped by one of the infected we had shot. He pulled out a pocket knife and a Petri dish from his pocket and took a fresh sample back to the professor.

It made me feel a bit sick. It was strange. I didn't mind shooting the bastards, but watching George carefully cut into the host and pull out skin, tissue, muscle and membrane, made my skin crawl.

As soon as everyone was safely inside we made our way back into the hangar, just as Flight Sergeant Tanner gathered everybody together.

"Okay, we're making good progress on the fencing. Once we've secured both bases we have some decisions to make. I need a team based here and another based over there. The choice is yours."

It felt good having a bigger base. I didn't care which side I went on, as long as it wasn't the same side as Duckface. I had spent over a month with her day after day; I'd had enough. She needed to go, or I did. Worryingly, I think Andy felt the same as I did.

"I'll move to the other base," Andy offered out the blue.

Duckface looked livid. "Um, excuse me," she said getting back on her high horse. "What if I don't want to go to that base? You can't decide for the both of us without consulting me."

Here we go again, I thought. I was already beginning to feel awkward.

He turned and looked her dead in the eyes. "I didn't say we would move. I said I would. Stay here if you want, I've got no problem with that at all." Andy gritted his teeth as he spoke. "Besides, what stops me from making decisions for the both of us? You do it all the time."

"I do it for us. Whenever I've made decisions for the both of us, it's because it's the right thing to do. It's always been for your own good," she spat.

Clearly reaching boiling point he glared at her. "If that's the way you want to play it, this is for your own good," he said, sticking his middle finger up at her, right in front of her face. He walked off without saying another word.

That was it; she snapped. She pulled her wedding ring off and flung it at his head. "I want a divorce!" she screamed. Her aim went wide and hit the floor to the side of him. She was always so full of drama; I'll give her that. She certainly knew how to throw a tantrum.

He turned around. "So do I! I've had enough of your bullshit. You're a control freak; I've spent most of my time here defending you and making up excuses for you. But what's the point? You're just a spoilt little selfish bitch, who's made my life a misery for the past four years!" he yelled.

She stood for a moment in shock at what she was hearing, as we all turned to look at her. She was shaking with anger; a vein was nearly popping out of her head. She had a face of pure evil as she glared at each one of us before she stormed off and went back into the plane. Nick and Paul went after Andy, probably to congratulate him. Lacey and I looked at each other with a huge grin on our faces. It was mean, but I couldn't help it. She had it coming for a long time. I wondered which of us would burst her bubble first and point out that finding a divorce lawyer in these circumstances may not exactly be straightforward. Although, I was proud of Andy. I had never seen him stick up for himself the whole time I had known him. She had finally pushed him too far and saw the consequence's at first hand.

Corporal Jameson came over to us. "Is anyone going to see if she's okay?" he asked us.

"Nope," Lacey and I replied in unison.

"Fair enough," he shrugged.

"Are you?" I asked as he turned to walk away.

"Hell no, that banshee scares the shit out of me," he said over his shoulder as he grinned.

"How's Andy?" I asked as Nick and Paul came back.

"He's fine," Nick responded. "He's gone up to the roof, he's offered to take watch. He just feels embarrassed to have caused a scene in front of everyone, so he's just going to cool off."

"So do you think this is it for those two then?" I asked him.

Paul nodded. "Without a doubt. He hasn't been happy for a long time. We've all seen it. Don't blame him, the poor lad."

I dreaded to leave the others as I made my way to the roof to make sure he was okay.

"Hi, Andy, mind if I sit with you?" I asked him.

"Go ahead, it's a free country. I'm sorry about that before. I didn't mean to make such a scene; I've just had enough."

I shook my head. "No, don't apologise. I think you've been holding it in for a while. We all knew you weren't happy with her. And none of us blame you. If I'm honest I'm surprised you've lasted this long," I joked, trying to lighten the mood.

"You're right. I'm surprised I haven't seen it until now. I've tried to make it work; I've let things slide so many times. But there's a line. She needs to grow up. Thinking back, I fell out of love with her a long time ago." He sighed.

I felt bad for him. He had put up with way more shit than he should have done. In a way it was his own damn fault, he let it get to this stage. If he had stuck up for himself in the first place, and not let her get away with so much, he wouldn't be in this mess. I could tell life was going to be awkward around the base. At the same time, if she wasn't such a control freak and didn't make him so miserable, he wouldn't have to flip out like he did. I couldn't wait until the fence was done; it was getting a bit too cramped in here.

The atmosphere that night wasn't pleasant. No one really knew what to say, so we spent the majority of the night in silence. Duckface didn't come out of her room, and we avoided her like the plague.

Andy spent the night on the roof. As it got late, Lacey brought him a blanket, but she couldn't get him to come down. We all figured he just needed some space, so we left him there. We went to bed early; we had a long day ahead of us, and the boys were already exhausted from building the fence. My shoulder was starting to throb again.

The next morning the boys loaded the truck, ready for another day of building. I went to the roof to set up our rifles as we had done the day before. Andy still hadn't come down, so, armed with a few energy bars I went up to take his breakfast to him. Meanwhile, the Professor offered to see to Lola. He was a brave man.

As I opened the roof hatch, I looked around towards the spot I had left Andy. I panicked at first – as I looked around I couldn't see him. I pulled myself up and onto the roof and spotted him in a corner wrapped up in the blanket. He was fast asleep. I let out a sigh of relief.

I made my way over to him, to gently wake him up. As I got closer, he opened his eyes. He looked dreadful.

"What are you doing here?" he asked, rubbing his eyes.

"I've brought you some breakfast, you've been here all night," I replied as I bent down, handing him the energy bars. "I think you'll need those. How are you feeling?" I asked.

"Like crap. But I want to get back to work. The sooner this fence is up, the better. I've had enough of this place." He groaned as he got up. With that, he trundled his way downstairs.

Poor guy, I thought to myself. Once I had set the weapons up, I made my way downstairs to see the boys off.

As I came downstairs, the professor was coming out of the plane shaking his head. As he got to the bottom Duckface emerged from the top.

"Will you all just fuck off and leave me alone!" she screamed.

I looked around at everyone. "Where did that come from?" I asked no one in particular.

"I don't want anything to do with any of you. None of you give a shit about me so stop pretending you do."

Oh dear, these were the tantrums I referred to earlier.

The Professor turned to face her. Saying completely calm he addressed her. "My dear, I am a scientist, not an actor. I simply came to you to make sure you were okay in yourself. Had I have not cared, I should not have bothered."

"Whatever," she replied. "I don't need any of you anyway, I'm fine by myself." She looked at us all in disgust. "You're all beneath me anyway," she muttered.

Typical Lola. Things don't go her way, it wasn't her fault, it was everyone else's.

I knew her kind streak wouldn't last very long. She always had an ulterior motive.

"That's enough, young lady." The Professor raised his voice. "I do not care for your tone one bit. You are acting like a spoilt child, grow up!"

"Fuck you!" she snapped.

The Professor's blood was now boiling. "Now you listen to me, child. You say these people are beneath you? Well, I'm sorry to say, you are beneath them. They have one thing you will never possess."

She laughed sarcastically. "Oh yes? And what might that be, Professor? Blood on their hands, dirt, no class?" she sniggered.

"Integrity," he replied, matter-of-factly. "That is something you'll never have. Not until you learn to act like an adult. All these fine people have a lot more class than you'll ever have, and I won't stand for this behaviour any longer. Now get out my sight." He scalded.

With that, she turned and left. The Professor composed himself. He turned to see us all staring wide-mouthed at his outburst. "Carry on." He smiled as he wandered back over to his makeshift lab.

Lacey and I made our way to the roof. We both had massive grins on our faces.

"Didn't expect that from the Professor."

"I know, she got told," Lacey giggled.

I couldn't deny it, watching that display had made my day. I had no idea why she lashed out at all of us; we stayed well clear of her after the argument between her and Andy. What did she expect us to do? Lacey must have thought the same as me.

"She probably expected us all to gather round her and make a huge fuss of her. I think she's upset because we just left her alone and didn't bother with her," Lacey suggested.

She was spot on, and I couldn't agree with the Professor more. She was acting like a complete spoilt child. She wasn't getting her own way, and we had all wised up to her behaviour, refusing to pander to it. She responded by throwing her toys out of the pram. Her behaviour was utterly ridiculous.

I put it to the back of my mind; I had more important things to deal with. Like the group of infected making their way towards the incomplete fence.

I pulled my rifle up and took aim, yet as I fired the first shot pain shot through my arm. I dropped my gun slightly, but ignored the pain as best I could. I carried on firing upon a small group. Lacey had spotted the same group, so she helped me dispose of them. As she looked over her shoulder, she turned her rifle and started shooting in the opposite direction.

I quickly disposed of the remaining of the group and focused my sights on the new herd coming towards us. Her aim was also improving considerably, although it did not come as naturally to her as it did me. In the distance, I could hear shots going off on the roof of Hangar 5. George had also spotted another group coming towards him.

They were all slow movers, none of them ran, they just stumbled along trying desperately to reach their prey. They all had limbs missing; organs and ribs were visible, as chunks of flesh and decomposing muscle had already been ripped out of them.

From out of nowhere, the fast movers came out running from all different directions closing in on the boys. The boys had all seen what was going on and had their guns at the ready. They had made themselves a makeshift cage, dragging the fencing they were working on in front of them. Directed by the flight sergeant they locked themselves in, for protection.

We needed to do something, there were literally hundreds of them. I shouted to Lacey, "Take out the fast ones, leave the groups for now!"

"Will do!" she shouted back.

I took control of the situation. I took down the fast movers as soon as they came into sight. There was too many of them, and they were advancing closer and closer to the boys. My shoulder was searing from the pain of the kickback from the rifle.

Shots were being fired from down below; the sprinters had closed in on the fence. The boys took them out as they came closer; some of them reached the fence, shaking the chains desperately trying to find a way in.

The airmen switched to their Glock 17s, taking them out from close quarters. The slow movers were getting closer. "Back on the groups!" I yelled.

We swung our rifles round, aiming for the advancing herds. "I'm out!" I yelled. I needed to reload quickly. We didn't have enough ammo with us to take them all down. I reloaded and emptied another magazine into another group of the slow movers.

"We need more ammo," Lacey called.

"I'm on it," I replied. "Take out the rest that come close to that fence. If too many get to them, the fence could fall," I shouted back to her.

I raced to the hatch, just as the professor poked his head out.

He was struggling to carry the boxes as he heaved them up to us. "I thought you girls might need a hand," he said.

I nodded and quickly took the boxes from him. I slid a box over to Lacey and reloaded my rifle as I headed back to my post.

I took out the last of the herds and concentrated on the fast movers. They were running from all different directions trying to find a way in.

The sprinters had a lot more body parts intact as they ran. They still had the diseased, rotting look of death. They were all covered in blood; I wasn't entirely sure the blood was theirs. They moved perfectly; they had full control of their movements. They had a crazed, murderous expression as they screeched a high-pitched sound. It was like listening to a crow being strangled.

The infected kept on coming. Bodies were piling up all around the perimeter; the stench of death was starting to make its way to the roof, and it was vile. After twenty minutes or so, we had disposed of them all.

Dead bodies, limbs and innards littered the ground beneath us. It was like a battlefield. We had taken out the enemy, and as far as I could see, we had no casualties.

My shoulder was still burning; I could barely move it. I lowered my rifle as I tended to my arm. A massage wouldn't fix it this time.

The boys started to make their way out of the makeshift cage they had designed for themselves. They wouldn't be able to carry on building until the bodies were moved. Flight Sergeant Tanner ordered everyone back to the base.

He gathered us all on the roof as he addressed us all. "Well, that didn't go quite according to plan. We need to remove of the bodies. Girls, I need you to cover us. We will move the bodies over there"—he pointed to the middle of the runway next to us—"We will pile them up and burn them all. Is that clear?"

We all nodded. I felt bad for all the boys. Those things stank. It wasn't a nice job at all, I knew I could never do it. I would need therapy for at least a year.

Sensing the disgust throughout the group, the flight sergeant added, "Don't worry, boys, we still have fully working showers in Hangar 5."

I let out a sigh of relief. If Nick came back smelling like those things, he was sleeping on the roof with Andy.

I watched with Lacey from above as the boys shovelled the bodies and innards into the trucks. They looked repulsed, but they carried on regardless. They loaded the first haul into the truck and drove it to the runway. Flight Sergeant Tanner lit the first pile and went back to load more.

It took them over an hour to dispose of all the bodies. The smell of burning flesh filled the air. I couldn't decide which I preferred, the smell of death raw or extra crispy. It was like being stuck between a rock and a hard place, trying to decide.

Once the bonfire was burning away, the boys finished off the fence. Once it was all done they retired to Hangar 5 for a much needed shower. We didn't see any more of the infected that day.

With the days events running through my mind, I was sure, without a shadow of doubt that the attack was staged.

My thoughts were confirmed in that moment, the infected were more than capable of carrying out a strategic attack, in fact, they already did.

Chapter 11

Moving Day

It felt better knowing we had more space to roam around. Once the flight sergeant had given both bases the okay, Lacey and I made our way to Hangar 5. All we knew about the hangar was from what Nick and Paul had told us. We were all keen to have a nosey, and see what we had to work with.

Lacey and I had decided we would move our living quarters to the second base. We both needed a change of scenery, and truth be told we wanted to stay as far away as possible from Duckface - especially given the new circumstances.

Nick and Paul were over the moon when we told them what we were thinking. They had both wanted to move with Andy anyway, so it suited them perfectly.

Josh and Greg wanted to stay in the main base, understandably they had spent far too long in Hangar 5, and weren't in any rush to go back.

The Professor and George had also decided to stay where they were; they had more space and wanted to move the rest of the lab equipment from Hanger 5 over to the bigger base.

Corporal Jameson moved over with us, so that Andy wouldn't be the fifth wheel, whilst Flight Sergeant Tanner stayed put. Not that we were complaining. Things were starting to come together nicely.

Duckface kept to herself, she barely left her room anymore.

To give my aching shoulder a break, George positioned himself on watch duty. I think he liked being back in action, there was no doubt about it; he still had a wicked shot. He spent most of his early life in the RAF. He often told us it was where he felt most comfortable, he was in his element being back in the game. I think he missed it, although he never admitted it.

After Lacey and I packed our things, we made our way over to the newly acquired base. The boys were already over there, eagerly setting everything up, making it a bit more homely.

I was so looking forward to having a hot shower. Although we had running water in the other base, it was always cold. We had to clean ourselves with cold wet towels most of the time. My hair hadn't been washed properly in so long, I couldn't wait to take it out of my high ponytail it was constantly in, and get rid of the dirt and grease properly that had built up over all this time.

As we entered the base we saw how much different is was from the larger base behind us. The large base we lived in for the past couple of weeks remained open plan. This base was split into multiple rooms.

The entrance to the base was obviously the garage. Spare tyres, various tools and even a hydraulic ramp stood in the centre of the room. To the side of the room, gym equipment was piled up in a corner.

We carried on through the door in front of us to the main hallway. Through the door on the left-hand side I could see Andy unpacking. It was a small room, enough to hold a single bed and a small cupboard. But at least he had his own room and some peace and quiet. We waved to him as we passed.

We still didn't know where either of us would be sleeping. I hoped that like Andy, me and Nick would still have our own room.

We carried on exploring our new home. The hallway carried on all the way down to the end of the building. As we passed Andy's room, another hallway to our left branched off. Lacey carried on towards the end of the building whilst I followed the other.

I came to a door on my right. I opened the door to find a small kitchen. There was a microwave, a fridge and a sink. It wasn't much, but it was ten times better than the non-existent kitchen on board the plane. We had to heat our MREs using these horrible pouch things called FRHs. They came in every MRE box and were designed to heat food out in the field; they made the food lukewarm at best.

The microwave was a much welcomed alternative. I was already looking forward to the luxury of a hot meal. We even had our own generator. I felt very privileged. This is what I had been reduced to. Before this stupid virus ruined everything, I had a very different idea of what the world 'privileged' meant. To me it meant owning a multitude of designer shoes and handbags, having a luxurious car to drive around in and a house with more bedrooms than people. Now, it meant a hot meal and a warm shower. How times had changed.

I closed the kitchen door as I ventured out once again into the hallway. Further down the hall on my right was another room. I looked through the window in the door, and saw the remains of the professor's lab. It wasn't as clinical as I had imagined, most of the equipment had already been taken to the other base, so it looked more like a classroom than it did a lab.

I glanced to the door on the opposite side. This, for now, was my favourite room. It was the shower room. It was very basic. Showers lined the walls at the centre of each cubicle. There were around twelve cubicles all lined up. Opposite the showers was a line of twelve sinks, each against a long mirrored wall. It reminded me of a public bathroom.

I looked at myself in the mirror; it was the first time I'd taken a good look at myself for a while. God, I looked rough. The days of wearing make-up were long gone. My hair was all over the place, I thought I'd snap a hairbrush in half if I attempted to put a brush through it.

I looked exhausted; my face was thinner but I had the biggest bags under my eyes I had ever seen. It was horrific. It looked as if I had completely let myself go. I stared at myself; it didn't even look like me. Thinking back to my old life, I never spent hours doing my hair and make-up; I much preferred to stay in bed as long as possible. But I always looked presentable. My hair was always neat and tidy, I never went out without make-up on.

I walked over to the full length mirror in the corner of the room. I was still wearing my home-made army outfit. I had definitely got skinnier. I was never fat in life; I always stayed a healthy size ten. I was now easily a size eight, maybe even a six. My waist had shrunk dramatically, the arm fat I always complained about completely vanished. My stomach looked a lot more toned, my legs were more defined. I was relieved I hadn't lost my boobs or my bum; in fact, my bum looked so much perkier than it used to be.

I felt strangely good about myself. All I needed was a shower and I knew I'd feel even better. I left the bathroom and went to find the others. More importantly I went to find my bag. I'd packed my shampoo and conditioner and, given the nest that was currently residing above my head, I'd need the whole bottle to tame it.

I made my way back to the main hallway and checked the rooms. I shouted to Nick. "Nick, where's our room?"

"In here, babe," he replied.

We had the room right at the other end of the base. Our room was obviously an old office. He had pushed the desk into the corner of the room and had made us a bed out of two camp beds pushed together. He had covered the beds in blankets, trying to make our new bed as comfortable and cosy as possible. He had already brought my bag to the room. I pulled nearly the entire contents of the bag out before finding my shampoo, conditioner and shower gel.

"I'm off for a shower," I told him.

"Don't forget your towel," he replied as he threw a brown, scratchy cotton towel at me. With that I ran back to the bathroom, eager to get out of my clothes.

I switched the shower on and started taking off my clothes. Looking in the mirror I could see the full extent of the damage the rifle had done to me. My whole shoulder was bruised. I could almost make out the shape of the rifle where it had dug in; it was all black and blue.

I quickly hopped into the shower, hoping the warm water would soothe it slightly. I stayed in the shower for nearly an hour. I had to put four lots of shampoo in my hair alone, before I saw a single bubble. The water was black as it washed away the dirt and grime.

Nick eventually came to look for me as I was taking so long. "Babe, you still in the shower?" he asked.

"Yeah why?" I asked.

"Well, it's been like an hour!" he shouted over the flow of the water.

He pulled open the cubicle door. "What the hell's happened to your shoulder?" he asked concerned.

"It's okay, it's just the kickback from the rifle," I told him. "I'm still getting used to it."

"Looks painful, maybe take a break for a while? Until the bruising goes down," he advised. He was cute when he was concerned about me,

I nodded. "Or, you could kiss it better for me?" I said, giving him by best 'come hither' look.

He looked around making sure no one else was around. "Okay." He smiled. He was already tearing his clothes off as he came in to join me.

* * *

It didn't take long for us to settle into our new surroundings. It already felt a lot more homely than our original quarters. We regularly visited both bases throughout the day, but went back to our own little communities at night.

The Professor remained, as always, hard at work. He was forever writing notes and adjusting the lens on his microscope. He worked off a laptop, powered by the main generator. His surroundings weren't the most advanced, but he did what he could.

George spent most of his time on watch, along with Josh. He was becoming a good mentor for the young private. George was full of old war stories; I was surprised at how interesting they were.

Corporal Jameson and Leon handled the training. They made sure we all carried on with our training on a daily basis. They spent an hour with each of us every day, we learnt hand-to-hand combat, how to handle different weaponry and they even gave us classroom training. We were turning into very good Rock Apes. I wasn't fond of the nickname, but George assured me it was a good thing. He told me to take it as a very nice compliment.

Andy seemed a lot better in himself. He put all his efforts into his training; the boys had turned the old garage into the gym. When he wasn't training with Jameson and Leon he was in the gym working out. I thought he wanted to get away from the tension between him and Duckface. They were rarely in the same room as each other. He was doing what he could to avoid her.

Like Duckface, Greg had started to keep to himself. He had turned very skittish, he didn't like to be around people, and he was turning into such a recluse. He started behaving very oddly. He gave up training and spent most of his time in his new room on the jet. He preferred to eat his meals alone in his room; we only got one-word answers out of him at best.

I heard stories on how soldiers who had left the force were often susceptible to mental illness due to the trauma they faced on the frontline. I hoped this wasn't the case, but it seemed the most likely cause. We had all seen our fair share of disturbing sights. This was worse than any war movie I had ever seen, and thanks to Nick I had seen pretty much all of them – or so I thought.

Truth be told, I never spent much time with Greg, so I had no idea what made him act this way. I spoke to Josh about him, and even Josh said that it was out of character for him. According to Josh he was always quite talkative, and very outgoing.

Josh had a theory that the infected shook him up, although he couldn't understand why.

"Who knows? He was fine when we were out there, he was shooting them all just like we were. He didn't shit himself or anything. He just got on with it," Josh told me.

"He started acting weird the day after all that shit happened. I reckon it all got too much for him and now he can't handle it. Happens to a lot of people, you know," he said.

I agreed with him, although I still thought there was more to it than that. Over the next day or two he started to rapidly decline. The odd times we saw him, he looked incredibly pale. It looked like he was coming down with the flu. No one else in the base felt ill, so I decided to speak to the professor about it."

"Professor, I want to talk to you about Greg," I started.

"No need, my dear," he replied calmly. "I saw him a few hours ago. I suspect this isn't just a case of the flu. I took a blood sample whilst he was sleeping. In a few minutes I should have the results. Whilst I was taking his blood, I noticed a small scratch on the palm of his hand. It looks to be an infection of some sort. Once I have the blood work back I can figure out how we can treat it."

"Is he turning?" I whispered to him.

"I'd say that's unlikely. I checked his body after I found the scratch. He doesn't seem to have been bitten. But we can't rule anything out at this stage." He lowered his voice.

I stayed with the Professor while he worked, until he checked the blood. He lifted his head from the microscope he was using and wiped his forehead. He rubbed his eyes before taking another look. I took it, this wasn't a good sign.

"Please, bring Sergeant Tanner to me," he whispered, looking up at me. I saw the fear in his eyes and the slight tremble in his voice as he spoke to me. I knew I didn't need to ask – our fears had just been confirmed.

I didn't argue as I rushed off to grab the flight sergeant. He was in his makeshift office on the plane. "Sergeant, please come with me, the Professor wants a word, urgently," I added.

He followed me back to the Professor. Jameson and Leon had spotted the professor and had wandered over to find out what was going on.

"Sergeant, I have just run a sample of Greg's blood. Please see for yourself the results." He motioned to the microscope. The Sergeant sat down to take a look. After a few seconds he stood up and took a step back.

"It's the virus," Tanner announced, taken aback. "Was he bitten?" he asked the Professor.

"As far as I'm aware, no he hasn't," the Professor solemnly replied. "However, he has a nasty looking scratch on his hand. I believe he may have come into contact with one of the infected when you were building the fence." He continued. "His health is starting to deteriorate, as the virus gets stronger. Right now his immune system is trying to fight it, hence the flu-like symptoms."

"So, why hasn't he turned?" Tanner asked.

"Well, I believe that as the scratch was small and quick, only a small dose of the virus got in. This being the case, his immune system is able to fend off part of the virus, prolonging the effects."

"What does this mean? Is he going to turn?" I asked the Professor.

"I think so. This is something I've never seen before so I can't be one hundred percent sure. Given the results of the blood sample, the virus is already embedded in his bloodstream. His immune system will continue to fight the virus, but eventually his body will shut down. When this happens the virus will fully takeover."

"How long do we have?" Sergeant Tanner asked.

"A day or two, tops," the Professor replied bluntly.

We looked around at one another, shocked and disturbed by the news. I felt sick. I hardly knew the guy but tears still welled up in my eyes. He wasn't going to be around for much longer. That I knew was certain. What do we do about it? Would we wait until he turned and shoot him like we did the rest – or would we shoot him now eliminating the danger before he became a threat to us all?

"What's your call, Flight Sergeant?" Leon asked.

The Sergeant stood for a moment and thought. "We ask Greg," he said, before heading off back towards the plane.

A few minutes later the flight sergeant came out, leading Greg to the professor.

"I'm infected, aren't I, Professor?" Greg asked. I saw the fear in his eyes.

"There's no easy way to say this, but yes," replied the Professor solemnly.

Greg looked around us all and fell to his knees. "I'm so sorry," he sobbed. "I should have said something, I was afraid this would happen. I didn't know what to do; I locked myself away. I tried to stay away. I don't want to hurt anyone."

He was a big man, he had a good heart but he was a proper lads' lad. Seeing him fall to his knees, he looked like a scared little boy. He was completely and utterly defeated.

I knelt down beside him. "How did it happen?" I asked.

He sat on the floor, wiping his eyes. "One of those fuckers got to the fence beside me, it got its hand through the fence and grabbed me. I pushed it off me and was about to shoot it, when its nail scratched through my hand," he said holding his hand up. "After the fight was over I scrubbed my hand trying to get as much shit out of it I could. But it was too late. The damage had already been done." He started sobbing again.

The flight sergeant knelt down beside him. "What do you want to do, airman?" he asked.

Greg looked up. He scrambled off the floor and bolted for the roof. "The only thing I can do!" he shouted as he ran. I was worried, he wasn't in his right mind.

We all ran after him, Leon was only a few seconds behind him and catching him up. We were a few paces behind. The Flight Sergeant was screaming for him to stop.

We got to the roof a few seconds too late. He was stood on the very edge, facing the ladder. "I'm sorry, I've let you all down. Please forgive me," he said tears streaming down his face.

"Don't do anything stupid," Leon said making his way slowly towards Greg.

"Goodbye," Greg answered as he leaned back.

"NOOO!" Tanner shouted, running towards the edge, trying to stop him. It was too late.

We all heard the crunching of bones as he fell to his death. I buried my head into Jameson's chest. I had never seen anything like this before. I was so shocked I was shaking. Sergeant Tanner and Leon leaned over the rooftop. I couldn't hear the words exchanged between them, but I could tell from the body language it wasn't good. My tears began to flow as Jameson gently comforted me.

Chapter 12

Securing the Base

The flight sergeant called us all in for a meeting. "It is with deepest regret, I must inform you all of Greg's passing. He was a good man and a great soldier. He developed the virus whilst out on the field. He gave his life so our lives would be spared. He didn't want to put us all in any danger. He will always be remembered." He spoke solemnly.

Duckface rolled her eyes, it didn't go unnoticed. I couldn't believe it. In all this time, she hadn't lifted a finger, and now she didn't even seem to care that Greg had lost his life. I bit my tongue, but inside I was infuriated.

It was wrong to think so, but I had wished it was her. Inside I knew, if she was ever to get infected, she wouldn't have sacrificed herself. No, she would have killed us all.

We all sat in silence for a few minutes, paying our respects. I felt numb. I had killed countless numbers of the infected; it got to the stage I had forgotten they were once people. Greg's passing had brought a new light to the situation. We had to be extra careful. It wasn't just the bites that were fatal; scratches were too. We needed to stay as far away from the infected as possible. The threat was becoming even greater as time went on. I was beginning to regret not spending more time with Greg. Maybe if I had taken the time to get to know him better, I could have stopped him. I knew it wasn't my fault, and I understood why he made the choice that he did. Regardless, I still had the whole 'what if' plaguing my thoughts.

Flight Sergeant Tanner finally broke the silence. "We need to get back to business. We will no longer stay confined to our bases. We survived for a reason. Greg did not give his life so we could spend ours cowering from the world. We are all soldiers now, and we are all going to act like it." He looked around at each and every one of us.

"Prepare the vehicles. I want this whole base cleared TODAY. I want to find out where exactly the infected are coming in from. Once we find their entrance I want it blocked off." Tanner ordered.

"Flight Sergeant, how do you know they're coming in from outside?" Leon asked.

"When the infected staged the attack, I recognised very few of them. Most were civilians, ones that we hadn't rescued," the flight sergeant admitted.

He was right. The attack on the base was most definitely staged. The runners didn't come out until the last minute. The slow-moving groups were coming from all directions; it was way too convenient. I don't know how they did it. But they were certainly showing signs of intelligence I never thought possible.

"I want two vehicles to sweep the area. I want everyone armed to the teeth. Any sign of the infected, you shoot. Aim for the head. We move out at 1600."

We had just under an hour. The boys split into two teams. Lacey and George started to make their way back onto the roof. I was about to join them, when I stopped. I had spent far too long on that roof. I hated seeing the boys in danger, when I was perfectly safe. I wanted to go with them. I hadn't left the confines of the base in weeks. I knew I had a good shot, plus I would be safe enough in the car. Besides, Lacey and George could easily cover us from above. I was curious to understand these creatures better. In order to do so, I needed to conquer my fear of them.

After thinking it over, I approached the flight sergeant, "I'm coming with you," I told him bravely.

He studied me for a while, "Are you sure you wouldn't prefer to scope from above?" he asked me. I shook my head. "Fair enough." He shrugged. "Arm yourself, quickly."

"You can ride with me," Corporal Jameson said as he handed me a Glock. "Is that it?" I asked him. He smiled and took a step to the side. Behind him was a line of assault rifles, grenades and submachine guns. "I'll take that one," I said pointing to the L85-A2. It looked heavy, but it came with its own arm strap.

"Nice choice," he replied as he made his way to the driver's seat.

Nick came over to me. "What do you think you're doing?" he asked, clearly annoyed with my choice to venture out.

"I'm going with you," I told him sternly.

He looked at me, a mixture of panic and frustration washed over him. "I don't want you to go anywhere," he said stiffly grabbing my arm.

I pulled my arm loose. "Babe, I'll be fine, I'm a big girl I can take care of myself."

His expression changed. He looked upset. I knew he was worried about me; he didn't want me in any danger. But it wasn't his choice it was mine. "Okay, be safe," he said defeatedly. He kissed me on the head. He knew this was a battle he couldn't possibly win. I was very stubborn. Once I had made my mind up about something that was it. No one was going to change it.

Nick headed off to join Andy and Paul, clearly still not overly impressed by my choice. Leon and Josh went over to choose their weapons.

I wandered over to the front of the truck; I opened the passenger door as Leon came around the side of the van.

"What do you think you're doing getting in the front?" Leon joked.

I looked at him and smiled. "Shotgun," I replied coolly, pointing my heavy assault rifle his way.

"Can't argue with that, mate," the corporal laughed as I climbed into the front seat.

"Try not to hurt yourself," he sniggered as he go in the back.

We started by driving around the outskirts of the base checking out the area around us. We didn't see any of the infected at all. The further out we drove, the more greenery we saw. It was stunning. Glorious green fields spanned for miles, completely untouched by the modern world. The weather outside was cold and crisp. We were in early October, so the leaves were just starting to fall off the trees, turning the leaves a lovely golden bronze. They crackled as the cold breeze ran through them. There were no more buildings around us, just the concrete runway.

The afternoon sun would soon be starting to set.

"The perimeter looks secure so far," the corporal announced. I carried on gazing out the windows. The whole base seemed so quiet. As we carried on around the base, we got to the back end of a business park. Still nothing could be seen or heard. We slowed down as we checked the fencing, making sure there were no gaps. All was secure.

We did a full circle, until we came to the main base. It was still on total lockdown. The base itself was huge. The building must have been at least a mile long and a mile wide. I shuddered as I thought back to all the people trapped inside, all infected. We drove all around the building.

"How many people were inside there when it got locked down?" I asked Corporal Jameson. He looked at me, his face pained by the memory. "At least a thousand," he replied sadly. "We did what we had to do" he went on. "There's no way they can get out, don't worry."

He pulled the truck around to the main entrance. There was a small crowd of the infected gathering, alerted to our presence. They were pushed up against the reinforced entrance trying desperately to reach us.

Leon banged on the roof.

"What do we do Jameson? Shall we take them out?"

The corporal looked around and stepped out the truck. The flight sergeant had stopped behind us and was getting out the car. He looked at the corporal sternly. "Take them out," He ordered as he went to relay his instructions to the rest of the team.

Jameson looked at me. "Stay in the truck, I'm leaving the engine running, I need you to stay on the lookout."

I did as I was told. I hadn't been this close to so many of the infected before. The smell was the first thing that hit me. Remember the smell when you open your outdoor bin, a day before the dustbin men come to remove it, and you find that the bags in there have all split? Well, imagine that smell mixed in with the smell of heavily blocked sewerage drains. Well, that doesn't even come close.

Flies surrounded the infected. Sores were protruding through their pale yellowing skin; some had already burst, dripping yellow viscous liquid down their faces. Signs of decay were present; parts of the skin not covered in sores looked as if they were being eaten alive from the inside.

Looking into the eyes of the infected would give me nightmares for weeks after. The corneas were completely red; the pupils were dilated and had completely removed the iris. The areas around the eyes were covered in black veins, which in turn covered the whole of their faces.

As they snarled and chewed at the air, I could see that most of them had parts of the mouth missing. Holes caused by decay were tearing the muscle from their cheeks, revealing their teeth as they gnashed. The gums had all but gone, revealing the jawbone dripping with blood.

I was terrified. They looked so much worse up close. The desperation to get to us was frightening. I watched as body parts flew off into the air and into the emerging crowd as assault rifles and submachine guns cut through the flesh of our enemy.

They screeched and hissed as shards of metals pierced through their stronghold, leaving a path of death and destruction directly opposite the entrance.

It didn't take long for the boys to dispatch of them all. I sat back in the truck. Looking around at the trail of death that lined the road made my stomach turn. The innards of the recently departed both smelled and looked foul. Steam rose from the bodies as they laid to rest in the cold air.

Not forgetting about the mission the corporal jumped back in the truck. "Let's carry on," he said to me as he looked over, his expression completely normal. "Are you okay?" he asked me slightly concerned. I hadn't moved a muscle since the ceasefire stopped. I was still trying to take in everything that had happened around me.

"Yes, fine," I replied, quickly shrugging him off.

We continued the rest of our journey in silence.

We carried on around the perimeter of the fence, and we came to some smaller buildings. Most were derelict and served no purpose for the air force. They were clearly from the days of the War; the brickwork was crumbling, some of the structures had already caved in.

As we passed them, I noticed the road ahead was familiar. We were back on Old Hall Lane, on the other side of the fence. I remembered the emergency exit sign we had passed when it all came rushing back to me. "I know where they're coming in from," I told the corporal.

"What? Where from?" he asked, he sounded puzzled.

I directed him to the entrance we had come through when we first discovered the base.

"We closed the gate behind us once we got in. We made sure we did. But if those things can figure out a way to ambush us, I have no doubt in my mind they could figure out how to open a gate," I told corporal.

He agreed as we pulled up to the gate. It wasn't how we left it. The gate wasn't closed properly.

When we had entered the bar had been pulled right across. Corporal Jameson walked up to the gate for a closer inspection. He closed the gate properly and walked to the back of the truck. I stepped out the passenger side, to get a breath of fresh air. I was still shaken up by the previous bloodshed I had witnessed. I started to understand why Duckface didn't want to be a part of it.

"We do what we have to, to survive," Leon said as he strolled along side me, noticing my inner turmoil.

"It's not that," I told him. "It's the way they looked, they weren't people. Those things. Whatever they are, they're not people!" I wasn't making much sense, but Leon seemed to understand perfectly. My goal had been to conquer my fears, but instead I felt as if I was flooding it. These creatures were utterly terrifying. One wrong move could cost you your life. I wasn't ready to die, and I wasn't ready to see my friends die either. I felt the anger in me begin to rise. I hated that I was so scared. I hated what those ugly, rotting un-dead corpses had reduced us to. My thoughts of fear were replaced with anger.

I watched the corporal as he pulled out a metal chain from the truck; he was securing the gate so nothing else could get in.

As he wrapped the first coil around the gate, when suddenly a set of sprinters came running towards him. Without thinking, we all ran to the gate. Leon and Josh pulled out their handguns and started firing. I ran over to Corporal Jameson to help him wrap the chain into place.

More and more of the infected came pouring out the nearby golf club. To our right, the flight sergeant was racing towards us with the second lot of troops. He stopped short as they jumped out the car and started firing directly at the clubhouse. The sprinters kept on coming. The boys were taking them out as they got to the path in front of them. Yet they couldn't shoot all of them, as the infected managed to outrun the attack.

The sprinters were getting closer and closer to us as we finally locked the chain into place. We stepped back with seconds to spare as the first sprinter launched himself at the gate, pulling wildly at the chain.

He looked up at me and the corporal, his eyes filled with hatred. He knew what we had done; we had stopped their entry to the base. He let out an ear-piercing scream as he shook the gate angrily. The corporal placed a well-aimed bullet through his head.

More and more came out, all running for the gate, pulling eagerly on the chains. I reached for my handgun as my hands shook. I was terrified, seeing them up close was all the more disturbing. I was still trembling as I flicked the safety off. I took a deep breath and took two out, hitting them point blank.

The fear was starting to leave my body as the adrenaline took over. I tried to remember my previous rage.

As I took more and more of them out, already getting used to being in such close range of the danger, I climbed to the top of the truck with the rifle on my back. I pulled the rifle towards me and emptied the magazine into the crowd that was gathering below. I took four out with one quick burst. I cracked a smile. It was so wrong, but I was proud of myself. I almost wish someone was there to video it. Damn, I was a good shot.

When I was out of ammo, I jumped down. Ditching the assault rifle, I pulled the handgun out of its holster around my thigh. I emptied the remainder of my magazine into the crowd. Still, they kept coming.

I quickly pulled a new magazine out and locked it into place. Discarding the empty mag on the floor, I kicked it out my way and carried on shooting.

"Looks like we found the nest," the Corporal shouted over his shoulder.

Leon was the first to respond. "At least we're on the right side, this time!" he yelled back.

"Not for long, the gate's not gonna last much longer!" the corporal yelled back.

We all carried on shooting. I had already emptied four magazines; I was quickly losing patience. My Glock just wasn't getting the job done.

It was useless; there were hundreds of them, still scrambling out the building. We needed more firepower. We couldn't use explosives, we'd would risk blowing up the gate and the rest of the fencing around us.

I ran to the back of the truck and found the LMG's (Light Machine Guns). I quickly grabbed two and ran back to the team. I threw one over to Leon as I readied the other.

The corporal and Josh moved to our side, backing up as they carried on firing. Leon and I stepped forward. Making a quick calculation of the average head height of these things, I pulled the trigger.

My shots hit the first few targets, but the kickback of the LMG caught me off guard. My last few shots went over their heads.

I stopped firing and tried again, this time I aimed a little lower.

Fully prepared for the kickback, I steadied my weapon as I kept the LMG at a constant level.

Bullets shattered the skulls of the infected in front of us. They were packed so tightly against the fence that the dead remained upright as the infected behind them propelled them forward.

Blood, guts and pus coated the gate and the floor surrounding us. I knew the gate wouldn't hold for much longer. The infected continued to surge towards us, pushing the fallen closer to the front, squeezing them through the chains.

Corporal Jameson jumped into the truck, shouting out of the window as he started the engine. "Move out the way, I have a plan."

We quickly fumbled into action, we jumped out the way as the truck reversed into position.

We reloaded our weapons and jumped on the roof alongside him. "What do you want us to do?" I asked.

"Aim as far away as you can. We need to hit them from behind."

I knew what he was getting at. We aimed out and fired on the infected pushing their way into the crowd.

They started to fall. The pressure on the gate lessened.

A few minutes later they were all down. We looked at the massacre in front of us, and at the gate that was starting to lean in towards us.

"We need to do something about that gate," the flight sergeant sighed as he made his way over to us.

"We've got some extra fencing in here, flight sergeant," Leon suggested, referring to the back of the truck. "Yes use that. Fence the area off. I don't want anyone to use this gate again; there are plenty of other exits we can use. Block it off," he commanded.

It didn't take long for the team to have the area secured. I reloaded the weapons whilst they got to work.

The world was still in complete meltdown. But I wasn't going to resort to manual labour just yet. I wasn't very good with my hands, I didn't want to slow them down, that was the excuse I gave anyway.

Once the area was blocked off, we headed back to the base. We all felt safer knowing the base was secured. We had taken out over a hundred in one day, but it was starting to take its toll on our ammo supply.

The flight sergeant knew this too well, so had already given us another mission. We were to pay a visit to Hangar 3.

Night had begun to fall so we decided to leave venturing out again until the next day. As the darkness surrounded us, I headed back to our living quarters.

We had already unloaded the trucks and placed the weapons back into the ammo store. I was already tired from the day's events. I just wanted to go back and get food, a shower, and bed.

I wandered back to the small base; it was completely dark at this point, but the moonlight illuminated my path. It was a clear night. I could see the stars were twinkling in the night sky. I slowed my pace as I took in the spectacular view from above.

All was quiet around me; you could have heard a pin drop. Even so, I was starting to get the uneasy feeling that I wasn't alone. I looked all around the base, my eyes adjusting to the darkness around me. I couldn't see anything.

I quickly turned my head and looked behind me; I knew I wasn't alone. I couldn't see anyone at all. I stood still, like a deer in headlights; my gut was telling me someone was out there. Fear started to take control – I couldn't speak. I just stood there unable to move. It was completely irrational; I couldn't see or hear anything so why was I so scared?

I shook my head and wiped my eyes; I was just being silly. I blamed the day's events mixed with sheer exhaustion, for playing tricks on my mind. I was about to head back to the base, when something to the left of me caught my eye.

I turned around and looked towards the corner of the building I had just come from. A dark figure stepped out from the shadows and into the moonlight.

It made no effort to advance towards me; it just stood there staring. I stared back, trying to make out what it was. It didn't look human. Its back was hunched over, and its head was completely bent off to the side. Its arms and legs were completely disfigured; they seemed to move independently from the rest of its body.

The more I stared, the more of its features I was able to make out. The area between the nose and chin were completely mangled. The skin looked like it had been completely ripped off, revealing parts of its skull. Its flesh around its mouth had been completely removed baring its blood-soaked teeth. Chunks of flesh were hanging from its face, blackened puss oozed out from beneath the wounds.

Its eyes bore the hollowing resemblance of death, a face that hell itself would spit back out. It was calculating its options. Working out how to get in.

It still made no attempt to move. It never took its eyes off me. Its eyes were hollow. There was no emotion in its eyes, just death. I saw its eyes dart around the fencing. It was looking for a weak spot. The more I looked at it, the more familiar it became. The clothing, the hair, even the build. It was Greg.

I stood still a couple of seconds not sure what to do. I quickly made up my mind. I bolted for the smaller base and headed for the roof. I knew there was a rifle up there. I quickly pulled the ladders out and climbed up the roof hatch, scrambling to get to the gun. I threw myself on the ground at the edge of the building, ready to take my shot.

I scoped the area trying to find my target. He wasn't there. I checked the corner he came out from, nothing. I searched the area around the fencing, still, no one there. I ran to each corner of the roof, desperately trying to find him.

There wasn't a soul outside. I sat down trying to figure out what happened. I felt like I was losing my mind. I was so sure I saw him out there. I couldn't get his picture out my mind. Did I really see him? I was starting to doubt myself.

I felt like I was going mad. I gave up on the roof and settled on taking a hot shower. As I entered the shower room, already with my towel wrapped around me, I flicked on the shower closest to me. I was in a world of my own as I reflected on the day's previous events, and the disturbing creature in the shadows. I barely noticed the other shower running, or the pile of clothes by the far sink. I was still in my own little world when Jameson stepped out from his shower cubicle wearing nothing but a towel around his waist.

As soon as he saw me, he came straight over to me. He walked with the same confidence he had when he was fully clothed. I fumbled pulling my towel up higher, trying to cover my modesty. He smiled at me as he neared. "I'm sorry, I didn't realise anyone else was in here." he told me.

I smiled back. I tried to keep my focus on his face. I have to admit, he shad the body of a God. He looked like he belonged on a billboard of a Calvin Klein advert. He had a beautifully defined six pack. His biceps were perfectly toned.

"It's fine. I'm in my own world it seems." I replied looking to the floor. He pulled my chin up towards him. "I'm worried about you, are you sure you're okay?" he asked. He stared deeply into my eyes. I averted my gaze yet again.

"I'm okay, it's just been a long day, that's all." I shrugged him off. The way he stared at me, so longingly made me weak at the knees. He was exactly the type of man I go for. Brood, manly and protective. The knight in shining armour as cliché as it sounds.

The problem was, I already had a knight in shining armour, and I loved him so much. Nick was so loyal to me, and always treated me like a princess. He was good looking in his own right. He never struggled getting girls before me. I felt a pang of guilt as I thought of Nick. I felt so guilty just for looking at Jameson the way I did.

"If that's all it is." Jameson replied. "But if you ever need to talk. You know where I am," he finished.

"Thank you, Corporal Jameson." I replied as I stiffened. He gave me one last smile. "Call me Ryan." he said softly. With that, he walked back to his cubicle and grabbed his clothes from the sink top. He left me alone to have my shower in peace. I watched him as he walked away. I could see the outline from his rear end through his towel. Just like the rest of him, it was perfect.

I stepped inside my shower cubicle and flicked the temperature around. I needed a cold shower after that particular encounter. I wasn't stupid, I knew he was interested, and if I'm completely honest I was too. But I couldn't do that to Nick. As much as my body wanted to, and believe me it did, Nick deserved my full attention.

Chapter 13

Hangar 3

I never told anyone about my experience outside. I still wasn't one hundred percent sure it was real. I had shrugged it off as my mind playing tricks on me. I did a quick check of the area the next morning, just to be sure. But I couldn't see anyone or anything out the ordinary.

We had more important things to concentrate on; we were going take back Hangar 3.

That morning, the flight sergeant handed us all two-way radios.

"What's with the walkie-talkies?" I asked.

He motioned for us to gather round as he spoke. "I've been working on our communications equipment. I have fully charged our two-way radios. From now on I don't want anyone to go out without them."

He carried on. "There's been a slight change of plan. I will be splitting the teams up slightly differently today. Team one will accompany me. Team two will accompany Corporal Jameson to Hanger 3."

He continued to split the teams. "Josh, Leon, Andy you will accompany me. The Corporal will take Nick, Paul and George to the hangar."

George? This made no sense. Why hadn't he included me in the teams? I had more than proved myself the day before. I had figured out the entry point, and my kill count was way above everyone else.

"What about me?" I asked him.

"You will be stationed back on the roof. Hangar 3 is still an unknown, and no one knows the area like George. I need him on this one, and I need you to provide cover," he replied.

I reluctantly agreed. He was right after all. It didn't go amiss that the flight sergeant had mentioned nothing of his team visiting the hangar. I pulled him up on it.

"And where will your team be going?" I asked quizzically.

"I received a faint distress call from the outside last night. Unfortunately, the signal was lost in the early hours this morning. We will be going to check it out," he told us all.

He'd been working on the communications equipment ever since we took over the base. By the sound of it, he had finally got it working, or part of it at the very least. I was still sulking about not being included as part of the ground team, but it seemed to perk Nick up.

"It's okay, babe, we'll be fine. We all know how well you did yesterday. Besides, you looked so hot shooting that MP5," he whispered as he squeezed my bum.

I wasn't in the mood. I was still confused about my feelings towards Ryan. I was trying my hardest to ignore them, the last thing I wanted to do was ruin my relationship with Nick. I reluctantly grabbed my rifle and made my way to the roof. At least I got to spend the day with Lacey. I had to admit, I did miss her whilst I was out the day before. We were already becoming inseparable.

We watched together, as the flight sergeant headed for the main base, choosing to leave through the main gate. Once they were out of sight, we turned our attention to team two; they were already at Hangar 3 and were making their way inside.

Our job was certainly a lot easier now we had secured the entry gate. We didn't see a single person, infected or otherwise that day. It definitely put me in a worse mood. I wanted to be in the action, not confined to the roof. It was boring. I wondered where the flight sergeant was going, and what sights he would come across along the way?

The boys seemed to have struck gold. They came in and out of the newly acquired hangar with boxes and boxes filled with new guns, explosives and ammunition. We would definitely be set for a while.

Once the truck was full, the corporal and the boys drove back to the base, ready to unload. Lacey and I made our way downstairs, both of us sick to death of sitting on the roof.

With the flight sergeant still gone, the corporal was left in command. Once the truck was unloaded, we all stopped for lunch.

"You know we've still got loads of fence left over," Nick said, gulping down his food. He carried on after he swallowed. "We could easily build another walkway into that other hangar. Then we'd have even more room."

"That's a fine idea, son," George agreed. "Did you know there is an underground tunnel system which runs through this base?" he asked as he carried on, clearly it was a rhetorical question. "Well, there's an entrance in that building," he said, pointing in the direction of Hangar 3.

"Where exactly does the underground tunnel lead to?" the corporal asked.

"It leads out to the middle of Isles Woods," he replied. "Just the other side of this base."

We all agreed we would build a fence and secure yet another base. We quickly finished our lunches and set about loading the fencing into the truck. As usual, Duckface refused to cooperate, instead creeping back into the plane. She was becoming such a recluse; she barely left the confines of that plane.

As the days went on, she had got less and less sociable. She had the worst attitude I had ever seen. She thought the whole world was against her since Andy dumped her. She had an almighty chip on her shoulder.

She refused to speak to any of us, only surfacing when told to by the flight sergeant or the corporal. She never spoke to the Professor and refused to acknowledge his presence when he entered the room.

As we were making headway securing more and more of the base, the Professor remained, as always, hard at work. Since Greg's death, he had gone into overdrive. Although he was his usual pleasant, normal self, I could tell that his death weighed heavy on the Professor's heart.

He blamed himself for Greg's death. Although he never confided in us, the way he buried himself in his work spoke volumes. He kept himself to himself a bit more with each day that passed. His only aim in life was to find answers.

None of us had any idea of what he was doing. People grieve in different ways; this was his way of dealing with it.

As soon as the truck was full the boys made their way back over to the hangar to make a start on the fencing work. Back on the roof it all was quiet. It was looking like we had secured the whole airfield.

Even so, the fence was an extra precaution. Always better to be safe than sorry. The boys carried on building into the night. With little danger around, it was worth risking it. Lacey and I had switched to night vision scopes so we could carry on watching over them, well into darkness.

By nine p.m. the fence was complete. There was still no sign of the flight sergeant or the rest of team one. As time went on and day disappeared into night we started to get worried, we didn't know where they had gone or what had happened to them.

We tried to get through to them on our radios, but they were completely out of range. I was worried about them all. What if something bad happened to them? They had been gone over twelve hours, where could they possibly be? I was nervous; all the worst-case scenarios kept running through my mind.

I knew they could all handle themselves, but what if they got ambushed? Or worse, ran into a horde of the infected? My mind was going into overdrive, I could feel the anxiety kicking in. I could have killed for a cigarette; I gave up a few years ago, but I wanted something to settle my nerves.

Thank God Nick hadn't gone with them; if he had, I would been an inconsolable wreck by now.

I decided to take a tour around the new building. I hadn't seen it yet, and I needed to do something to take my mind off the worry.

I made my way through the newly erected fencing. Ever since I thought I saw Greg, a few nights ago, travelling through the fencing made me jittery.

I kept a swift pace as I wandered over, trying to spend as little time as possible outside. My heart was pumping. Partly from my nerves due to the unknown fate of team one, and partly from my past experiences with the infected.

I opened the door to the new base and glanced around me. It was way too small to be considered an aeroplane hangar. Through the door on my left was a room the size of a gymnasium. Rows upon rows of green fold-out camp beds had been set up. The RAF must have set this up as extra living quarters for survivors. It was very basic. It looked like a shelter home.

Each camp bed had a brown folded blanket and pillow at the edge of the bed, confirming my theory.

On my right were large, keypad entry double doors, leading to another supply room. The doors were propped open, from the team's earlier raid, so I let myself in.

The room was slightly smaller than the room opposite, but not by much. Steel racking lined the walls; emergency backpacks still hung on the walls. I looked to my left, and I couldn't help but laugh. Nick had already moved his fishing gear in here; it was propped up against the wall next to the backpacks. I had completely forgot he took it with him, the sad bastard.

More fencing and barbed wire stood in the middle of the room. At least the air force was well prepared.

I wandered over to the next room, wanting to find the entrance to the tunnel George had spoken about.

I walked around the whole room, checking the floors as I went along. I couldn't find any opening at all. I could have easily asked George where it was, had I not wanted to discover it on my own accord.

I left like Indiana Jones, trying to find the lost temple. Only it was a tunnel I was looking for. And rather than searching the jungle, I was searching an old RAF base, in the middle of an airfield. Okay, so it was nothing like Indiana Jones, more like a modern day Sherlock, and Lacey was my Dr Watson, I chuckled at the notion of us solving crimes together, I doubted we would get very far.

After my second lap of the hall, and looking under all the beds, I gave up. I decided to check the supply room instead, positive that the entrance couldn't possibly be under any of the beds.

I wandered back into the supply room. Paying close attention to the floor around me, I started to search. It was a lot harder to search this room; the floor space was minimal. Empty crates and boxes filled the area.

After checking around the floor space available, there was nothing there. Positive that the door must be in this room I tried to move some of the boxes out the way to get a closer look.

Empty boxes littered the middle of the room; I started pushing them out the way.

The floorboards in the room had certainly seen better days, they were very old-fashioned, the closer in I got, the more careful I had to be. There were holes where the floorboards had snapped, sunk into the floor.

Just as I was moving the final lot of boxes, my heel got caught. I tried to pull my heel out, but it wouldn't budge. I threw the boxes down, irritated it was blocking my path.

I bent down for a closer look at the hole I was caught on. When I looked, it wasn't a hole. The heel of my shoes had got caught in a metal ring screwed to the floor.

I looked around me. The section of the floor I was stood on was slightly out compared to the rest.

I soon realised this was it! I had found the trapdoor. I quickly pushed the rest of the boxes out of the way.

After uncovering the boxes, I saw two steel hinges bolted to the floor. I knocked on the trapdoor; it was definitely hollow.

I pulled at the metal handle which had earlier wrapped its way around my heel. It was stuck. I pulled harder and harder putting all my weight into it. I felt it open slightly, but it was still jammed.

I stood upright and planted both feet on the flooring around me. I pulled the handle leaning all by weight back when it finally lifted.

As it opened dust flew back in all different directions, the force of the door pulling back made me lose my footing, I let go of the handle to regain my balance. As I did, I cracked my index finger nail and my thumb.

Perfect. This is exactly why I stay clear of manual labour. My nails were always in perfect condition, and they were completely natural. I didn't need acrylic or gel false nails, my nails were incredibly strong, they hardly ever broke off. Until now.

I shook my hand; the pain where my nail had split just below my nail bed started to throb. I quickly dismissed the pain, more interested in finding out what was underneath the door.

I looked down the pit in front of me. A timber-frame ladder led the way down. I pulled on the ladder making sure it was secure. I looked around trying to find a torch, when the familiar sound of a car engine approached.

I let out a huge sigh of relief. Team one was finally back. My yearn for adventure now subsiding as I hurriedly closed the trapdoor, I made my way back to the base to greet them.

As the team exited the car, I could tell they were all exhausted. They didn't bring with them any new survivors, and both they and the car looked like they'd seen better days.

They were covered in dirt. The car was dented and scratched; splashes of blood coated the wheels.

"What happened?" I asked as they stepped out.

"It's a long story," Leon replied hobbling out the car. "We're fine, don't worry, just a bit banged up."

The Professor came running over, his face a picture of concern. "Are you all okay? Have any of you been bitten or scratched? Have you come into contact with the infected?" He was bombarding them all with questions.

Flight Sergeant Tanner put his hand up to silence the babbling Professor. "Don't worry, Professor we haven't come into close contact with the infected."

The Professor looked relieved. "Okay, good... As you were, men," he nodded as he wandered back to his lab.

"Good to have you back." The corporal greeted the flight sergeant with a friendly handshake.

Andy was the last to get out the car. He was visibly shaken by the day's events. He looked like he had just been in a street fight. There was bruising around his eyes and face as he shakily pulled himself out of the car.

Chapter 14

The Search for Survivors

After they had all freshened up, team one joined us in the plane to fill us in on what had happened that day.

The following is the account Flight Sergeant Tanner and the rest of the team gave us. He explained the events to us in full.

*

As you all know, I received a distress signal from the communications box I have been working with. The call came from a young female. She said she had children with her, and was in need of urgent rescue.

I managed to communicate with her only once. I told her my name and that we were nearby. She told me her coordinates and the line went dead. That was the last I heard from her. When I lost contact, I immediately tried to re-establish the connection. When my attempts failed, I assembled the team.

She had made the call from Bramhall Hall, a stone's throw away from where we are now. Andy was familiar with the area and after I had approached him, he was keen to join the team. He told me it was in the middle of a woodland area not far from here.

We made our way to the Hall. We took the long way round, wanting to avoid the centre of the village. It is a highly populated area, and we needed to stay clear of the infected. We took the long way round, not wanting to draw any attention to ourselves.

I was apprehensive of spending longer on the road than necessary. But staying out of sight was by far the best option.

We made our way through Woodford, towards Poynton. We turned off down a country lane which led out to the main road, which I'm told leads to Hazel Grove. Andy kindly directed us to the park, which didn't take us long to find.

Before long we were at the entrance to the park. There were no sign of the infected, so we drove in. We were fully armed by the time we got to the house although our drive towards the manor was uneventful; the infected were nowhere to be seen.

As we pulled up, we all got out the car. I wanted to do a quick sweep of the area, just to be sure, so I sent Leon ahead to secure the area.

When Leon finally returned, there was an ambush waiting to greet us. Kids of all ages surrounded us. We were outnumbered ten to one.

I offered them a place with us, but they declined. They were all wielding knives and home-made bats, they knew we were coming and had planned an attack.

The team readied their weapons to attack, but I ordered them not to shoot. I wasn't about to have their blood on our hands. After all, they were still children. Who knows what horrors they had already faced, that drove them to this?

The leader emerged from the group. He was a young boy, no older than sixteen. He had a shaved head; he was tall but quite scrawny. He obviously didn't have the best upbringing before the virus took over, he was brutish and thug-like. The type of boy that would be in the runnings for a gang member as he got older.

The boy stepped forward and eyed us all. He turned to his crew members and with a grin he said, "Fuck 'em up."

The first lashed out and stuck Leon in the kneecap. As he fell to the ground, the others started to advance. I fired out some warning shots into the trees; they took a step back, but carried on when they realised we weren't shooting at them.

We defended ourselves as much as we could; I didn't want to harm the children. We used our rifles as batons and managed to push them back and hold them off. But we were still outnumbered. We pushed our way out of the crowd but had no choice but to retreat into the woods.

The remaining kids, hiding in the bushes, took off with our vehicle in the attack. Luckily we were still armed.

We walked around for hours trying to find a way out. The kids had set up a perimeter; they had lookouts stationed at each post. They were very well organised. They had used the great hall as a safe house; they had claimed it as their own.

After a few hours we saw our vehicle return. Clearly none of the kids knew how to drive, the car was covered in dents and scratches, but it was still drivable. We needed to get the car back. As much as I wanted to help these lost boys, there was nothing we could do for them. They were already too far gone.

We hid in the nearby foliage and watched as they pulled a young woman from the car. She was tied up and gagged. They pulled her out the car and pushed her to the floor. As she scrambled to get up, the leader punched her back to the floor. She must have been a schoolteacher; I overheard a few of them call her Miss Robinson.

Leon pulled his rifle up to aim, yet I pushed the gun down. I wasn't prepared to shoot anyone living, especially a child, no matter how messed up they were.

Whilst we were busy watching the scene unravel before us, a group of infected came at us from behind the trees. We struggled to keep them at bay in the end we had no choice but to shoot, giving away our position.

We quickly dispatched the infected even as the group of boys soon surrounded us. Our cover was blown. We were outnumbered, and couldn't escape without causing serious injury to the boys, so we let them take us. We refused to give up our guns, but as they knew we wouldn't use them, they took them anyway. They took us to the house and tied us up; they locked us a room with Miss Robinson.

The room they chose for us was an old bedroom, there was a grand four-poster bed in the centre of the room, handcrafted from English Oak. The furniture in the room matched the bed perfectly; even the walls surrounding us were wooden panelled.

It didn't take us long to untie ourselves. They had neglected to take my pocket knife. It wasn't long before I manoeuvred myself free. I untied the others, including Miss Robinson.

She was terrified. She begged us to take her with us, which we were more than happy to do. She was a timid woman; she had a very pale skin tone and mousey brown hair. She wore glasses that were all bent out of shape. She didn't look like she was capable of hurting a fly, let alone being able to defend herself. But she needed our help, and we weren't going to let her down.

We calmed her down and promised to take her with us. We told her about our base, and that she would be in safe hands with us.

A thick heavy oak door blocked our escape. Even if we tried to knock the door down, we would alert the rest of the gang, and they would know we had broken free. For their sake and ours we waited.

After a few hours passed, the leader who Miss Robinson had earlier confirmed as a boy named Ben entered our room. He was extremely cocky. He had embraced and taken advantage of his leadership role. The lost boys didn't respect him or necessarily agree with him; they just did as they were told. They were most likely scared of him.

We heard him coming up the stairs. Before he entered I quickly alerted everyone, and we sat back down with our hands behind our backs. We were going to use the element of surprise.

He had a thick Manchester accent. He walked with an invincible strut. He had the attitude of I-can-do-what-I-want. He had no respect for his elders and only cared for himself. He had a loud mouth, everyone knew when he entered a room.

"Not so 'ard now are ya?" He looked at us all grinning. "We propa fucked use up out there, big bad army men rollin' up in ya bad man car," he spat. He grinned as he held the keys up to us. "Mine now, init?" he told us. The two boys behind him sniggered.

He pulled a handgun from his tracksuit, where it was tucked in behind his back. "This is mine too," he said holding it up for us all to see.

He walked over to Andy, bending down to his level. I could see Andy's fists tightening behind his back, the skin was starting to pale against his knuckles as he tried to control his anger.

"Was this yours, mate?" the boy taunted him. Andy didn't say a word. The boy flipped the gun around holding it by the barrel and struck Andy across the face. "Are you deaf or summit?" he shouted. Andy still didn't move.

"That's enough!" I shouted to the boy.

He turned and looked me up and down. "I'll tell you when it's enough, old man," he sniggered, dismissing the rest of us.

All of a sudden we started to hear the commotion outside. Screams and shouts could be heard in every direction. It seemed the lost boys' cover was blown.

The infected must have been alerted to our gunshots, and our car they'd been recklessly driving around. We heard the car whilst we were locked away. The boys were revving the engine; to the infected they may as well have been ringing a dinner bell. They were quickly approaching the manor house, coming in from all directions.

I could hear gunshots as the lost boys attempted to fend off the infected.

"Close that door, quick!" Ben quickly motioned to the other two boys. They did as they were told. They fumbled with the door but quickly locked it into place. As they turned around I noticed they had our other two handguns tucked into their trousers, exactly as their leader had done.

We listened as the battle continued. We heard gunfire, as the other boys attempted to ward off the horde of the infected gaining rapidly on them.

I heard the boys shouting for help. "Ben, we're being attacked, help us!" they screamed from below. Their leader made no attempt to acknowledge them, let alone help them.

"Fuck, there's shit loads of them out there," Ben told the two others.

"Are you not going to help your friends?" I asked him.

"Nah, fuck 'em, we're all right in 'ere. Not going out there, fuck that," he responded coldly. Beneath his cool exterior, I could tell he was as scared as the rest.

We heard the door slam. They had retreated inside. We heard glass smash from beneath us as the infected forced their way inside.

Seeming slightly shaken to the new threat outside the leader continued to threaten us. "If any of use make a noise, I'll shoot you in the head, swear down I will."

"Oh, I don't doubt that for a second," I responded, staying calm. "You left your friends to die out there, if you can do that, you are more than capable of pulling that trigger."

"Shut up, int my fault what's going on outside, you don't know me," he hit back, aiming the gun for my head.

Miss Robinson started to cry. We all kept our hands behind our backs.

"Stop crying, stupid bitch!" the boy shouted. "Shut the fuck up!" He was now pointing the gun at the middle of her head.

I'd had enough. I sprang into action pulling the gun from the boy nearest to me. Aiming my newly acquired weapon at the boy, I shouted for him to put the gun down.

The second boy tried to scramble for his gun, but Leon was quick to respond, knocking it out of his hands before he had a chance to do any damage.

"Ben! Give me the gun," I told him.

He looked at me; he was down, but he certainly wasn't out. "Fuck off! No. Give him the gun or I'll shoot," he said, pointing to one of the other boys. His gun was still firmly attached to his former teacher's head.

"You don't want to do this. Give us the gun, and we'll all get out of here," I asked him calmly.

"No, don't even try telling me what to do," he said, his voice was filled with anger.

"Ben, mate, just do as he says, it's not even worth it," One of the boys piped up, obviously starting to see sense.

"Listen to your friend," Leon told him. "It's over."

"NO!" he screamed as he pulled the trigger.

Miss Robinson slumped back. Blood covered the young boy. He turned to aim the gun at us, his face of pure evil. I quickly shot him in the kneecap. He fell down dropping the gun. He screamed in pain as the searing bullet pierced through his skin, shattering his kneecap as he fell.

I had no choice. He would have shot us all if I hadn't acted.

With their leader down the two remaining boys made a hasty retreat. They didn't get very far. The infected were already inside the building. They ran straight into the open arms of the infected. They were ripped apart within seconds.

The boy was bleeding out fast. We tried to help him up, but he was having none of it.

"Get the fuck off me, you wankers!" he yelled, pushing us away from him.

There was nothing we could do for him. We did what he said; we left him in the room, just as the infected made their way up the stairs.

We had three handguns between the four of us. We had lost the rest of our rifles and ammunition when we were held captive.

The whole manor was a bloodbath. Groups of the infected feasted on the children. Screams could still be heard in the distance. Some of the boys must have fled into the woods to escape. Judging by screams and the cries for help, they hadn't got very far either.

The battle was over. The boys had lost; the infected had taken over leaving nothing but death and destruction in their path.

We fought our way out the building, but when we got out we realised we didn't have the keys to the car. I was kicking myself when I realised we had left them in the pocket of the former leader, Ben.

We had very little ammo left, and the infected were still roaming around the house. We had no choice; we made our back way to the building, and to the room we had just come from.

We maneuvered our way up the stairs, stepping over the bodies of both the lost boys and the infected.

As we got back to the room, we saw that the infected had already descended on the body. Using my last few bullets I took them out, one by one.

He was already dead. Blood poured out from his wounds. His neck had been ripped off; flesh hung from his body. His stomach had been torn out, and his organs were now visible encased in blood. It wasn't a pretty sight. His eyes, still wide open, showed the pain and suffering he endured in his last few moments.

I leant down next to the boy and checked his pockets. It didn't take me long to get a grasp on the keys. I quickly yanked them free and closed the young boy's eyes. I put a bullet through his head before I left. Just to make sure he wouldn't awaken in an altered state.

We all sat there, wide-eyed as Tanner revealed the day's events. It brought a shocking realisation back to us, on how bad things were out there.

Chapter 15

Communications Centre

Much to my surprise, the flight sergeant insisted on keeping the communications with the outside world open. In his eyes the trip, although not quite according to plan, had proved successful. They were able to confirm that there were indeed survivors out there and that they were still alive, no matter how fucked up they might be.

This started to cause a divide within the group. Given the hoax call and the danger the team was in, not everyone was overly keen on inviting new people to our safe haven. Duckface was enraged with his decision. The thought of 'unsavoury guests' darkening our doorstep had not gone down well with her, at all.

She wasn't the only one to turn her nose up; Leon wasn't convinced and neither was Josh. Although they didn't agree with the decision, neither of them dared question the flight sergeant. The corporal also had his doubts, but still remained optimistic.

I didn't really know what to think. We had the resources to help people, but how on earth would we go about finding them? And how do we know they want to be found? Are they worth putting one of our own at risk?

All these questions kept whizzing through my mind. I didn't have an answer to any of them. The more I thought about it, the more positive I became. It's very easy, in a situation like this, to presume the worst. To lock yourself away from the outside world, and even pretend it's not there.

Duckface was a prime example. She was full of negativity; she was very bitter. She let the negativity surround her, and was starting to let it spread to the others. Her outlook on life was very bleak. She did only what suited her, she was very self-centred. She didn't care if the people outside lived or died, they were of no importance to her.

I decided very quickly that I didn't want to end up like her. I had to put my trust in Flight Sergeant Tanner, and believed that what we were doing was for the greater good. I asked myself, what would I do if I was out there? The answer was clear. I would do what I could to survive, and hold out hope that I would be rescued.

I knew the flight sergeant and the corporal wanted to rescue others, perhaps to make up for the lives lost in the main base. The flight sergeant had made that decision for the greater good. To secure what was left of the base, and to provide refuge to future survivors. I understood his reasons perfectly. He sacrificed his family and his men for his beliefs. I would help them both; after all they took us in when we landed on their doorstep. They made sure we had a roof over our head, food, water and even training. For that, I was extremely grateful.

The flight sergeant didn't want to waste any time getting back out. He sent the boys out on a daily basis, scouring the nearby areas. They stayed away from town centres, sticking mainly to the country roads and the outskirts. Tanner stayed firmly connected to the radio frequencies.

As usual, I stayed on the base. We never saw any of the infected around the base. As far as we were all aware, it was safe. We barely used Hangar 3. Our ammunition didn't have the chance to deplete, now there was no threat. All was quiet and peaceful on the base.

Day after day they returned empty handed, they occasionally came into contact with the infected, but were yet to find any survivors.

I was apprehensive the first time Nick went out. After the flight sergeant had told us what happened that day, I didn't have much faith in the outside world. I wanted to, but I knew I had to be realistic.

The sergeant spent most of his time on a new project. He wanted to get the satellites working again. Greg was the communications engineer, without him things were certainly proving more difficult. The Professor put his research to one side and helped the flight sergeant with his project.

They had a set-up on the roof. Within a few days, the satellite signal started to pick up. Our mobile phone signals were starting to come back. Very slowly we were able to access the Internet.

Duckface slowly started to come out of her room. One morning, during our daily meetings in the dining room, she had handed over her phone, and explained to the flight sergeant about the group she had created on Facebook.

"The E-Virus Support Group?" he asked.

"Yes, it's how we found this place, someone put down that they had heard it was safe," she replied.

"Okay, I'm sorry I don't quite understand Facebook, I've never used it, nor have I had any intention. Please go on," he told her.

She proceeded to tell him all the ins and outs of Facebook. I could see his eyes glazing over, but bless him, he still listened.

When she finished babbling on, he had a look for himself. He looked up in surprise. "The last post was three days ago," he told us all.

Wow, I was surprised people still had Internet access. It seemed that, even in our darkest days, Internet was still possible. The post simply read:

QUELQU'UN EST-IL LÁ-BAS?

"What the hell does that mean?" I asked.

"It's French I think, hun," Lacey replied.

We soon found out it was written by a French national called Claude Zidane. After a quick Google Translate it read:

Is anyone out there?

They obviously weren't here in the UK, but it was a good sign, it meant there were people in other countries still alive, and had access to the Internet.

It was rather ironic that, even with the world falling apart, Facebook was still the most common communication method throughout the world.

"This is very good Lola, are you able to continue communications? It seems like the best way for us to locate fellow survivors," the Sergeant asked.

Duckface looked around the room, her expression clearly showed her reluctance. She still didn't like the fact that we were inviting strangers into our base. She was worried they wouldn't be 'her sort of people.' Her arrogance had no limits.

Despite her feelings towards newcomers, she reluctantly agreed. To make sure she wasn't going to withhold any important information, the flight sergeant made a point in checking the page daily as well.

We had all decided collectively not to give our position away. Given the incident with the lost boys, it was safer keeping ourselves hidden. We didn't want to attract any unwanted attention. Duckface seemed a lot happier with this.

Whilst Duckface immersed herself in her new communications role, Andy started to keep more to himself. He trained harder than ever; we all saw a big change in him.

He went out with every team that ventured into the outside world. He didn't seem to like being stuck inside, he went out at every opportunity.

I never ventured into the outside world. Part of me wanted to, I had been keeping up my fitness regime, but I didn't know what it would be like out there. If I got into danger, I don't know if I had quick enough reactions. The infected were things out of nightmares; they terrified me. What terrified me even more was the thought of ending up like that. I didn't want to put myself, or anyone else for that matter, in any danger.

Things were starting to get boring around the base. With no immediate danger, we struggled to find things to do.

After a conversation between Lacey and I, we decided to revisit the tunnel. The curiosity started to get the better of us, and we needed an escape. With Duckface licking the flight sergeants arse every time we turned around, we needed a breather. She was so wrapped up in her new role, she was on a power surge.

We made our way over to Hangar 3. No one usually ventured over, there wasn't much in there apart from the emergency camp beds and supply room.

I entered the supply room and made my way over to the trapdoor. Remembering my previous struggles and broken nails we pulled open the door together. Grabbing a few torches from the emergency supplies, we pointed them down the dark hole.

The smell was the first thing that hit us. A damp, earthy smell made its way to the surface, along with a chilling breeze that made us both shudder.

The wooden ladder looked stable enough; it had been there a while, but it was solid wood. I made my way down the steps first. As soon as my foot hit the concrete floor, Lacey started to make her way down.

The whole tunnel was pitch black; only our torchlight illuminated our path. The tunnel was much bigger than I expected. The concrete walls circled their way around, going off in all directions. It was so easy to get lost.

We decided to investigate the main tunnel only. The last thing we wanted was to get lost or trapped down here. We had to sneak off in the first place; George didn't want anyone to go down there.

"This place is huge!" Lacey exclaimed, her voice echoed through the tunnels. She giggled as her voice carried down the tunnel.

I whispered back, "Shhh, you'll cause an avalanche."

She started giggling again "You only get avalanches in snow, I think we'll be fine," she whispered back.

I started to laugh with her; I was always getting my words wrong. We made our way through the underground passageway shining our torches in all directions. It was deathly silent all around us, the sound of dripping water somewhere in the distance, along with our footsteps, were all that could be heard.

I felt like an explorer discovering the winding passageways of the Pyramids. Well, I would have done, had it not been so cold.

There was a definite breeze pushing past us. "There must be an opening around here," I told Lacey. "That breeze has to be coming from somewhere."

We carried on down the passageway, eager to find the source. It was still pitch black in front of us when Lacey stopped me.

"Did you hear that?" She asked, slightly concerned.

I stopped for a minute trying to listen out. "Hear what?" I asked her.

"That rustling over there." She pointed her torch in front of us. "I swear I just heard something."

I stopped again trying to listen out, but I couldn't hear anything. Still, I was starting to get a little jittery. We'd brought our handguns with us; I slowly pulled mine from its holster.

We carried on, tiptoeing our way forward, more aware of our surroundings. This time it was my turn to stop.

"I just heard it," I whispered. We both stood there, not sure what to do. We switched our lights off as the rustling got louder; it was coming closer.

With our guns raised we quickly turned our lights back on. We pointed the light ahead. We couldn't see a thing; nothing was there. We looked at each other, both equally perplexed at the strange noises, when the rustling started again.

This time it was coming from behind us. We turned around slowly, guns at the ready. Again we couldn't see anything out of the ordinary.

We were starting to get freaked out. We were both hearing the sounds, but yet we couldn't see anyone. We decided to head back; we'd had enough excitement for one day.

As we turned to leave, I felt something brush past my feet.

"What the fuck was that?" I jumped back, grabbing onto Lacey's arm.

We aimed our torches down quickly.

"Oh my God, RATS!" Lacey screamed

There were three of them, and they were absolutely massive, easily the size of a cat. They were scurrying around our feet, running away from the light. Watching their thick wormlike tails following behind them made me jump back. I hate rats.

We both shrieked and ran back to the base, as fast as we could. We didn't look back; we just kept running. We were both horrified. When we were nearing the ladder, a loud noise stopped us dead in our tracks.

It was an ear-piercing scream, followed by a gunshot. And it was coming from above.

We looked at each other, panicked. We darted back upstairs, our guns still in our hands. We had already completely forgotten about the rats. We threw the trapdoor back down and raced back towards the base.

We didn't have to get very far. As soon as we ran outside, we saw what happened. Duckface and Andy were stood, both of them in shock, looking at the dead body before them. Andy still had his gun aimed at the body, as if he was waiting for the corpse to move.

I couldn't see very clearly at first. They were both stood over the top half of the body, but I could see clearly the combat trousers and boots belonging to the recently deceased. By this time, the flight sergeant and the rest of the group were running out, to see what all the commotion was about.

As I edged closer, I gasped. It was Greg. Or rather it used to be. His face was covered in blood; his skin was rotting and puss oozed from the sores and boils forming on his arms and neck.

There was no doubt about it; he was infected. What was more worrying was that he was on the inside of the fence, not the outside. Somehow, he managed to get in.

I couldn't believe it. I wasn't seeing things after all. I thought back to the night I saw him. His bones were all disfigured. Looking down on this corpse, there were certainly differences. His body wasn't as out of place as when I first saw it. I could see where he had broken bones; however, they were nowhere near as severe as what I saw in my first encounter.

"What happened?" Flight Sergeant Tanner demanded. We all looked up; he was as shocked as the rest of us, yet he was trying to keep hold of his calm demeanour.

Duckface was as white as a ghost; she took a few steps back and ran back to the base. No one made any attempt to follow. We were all fixated on the body laid out before us.

"Well?" The flight sergeant asked.

"I don't know what happened, we weren't here. We heard a scream and a gunshot from inside and ran out here," Lacey said defensively.

Andy looked up. He threw his gun to the ground. "I saw Lola leave the base, she was headed this way, probably to find these two –" he looked to us. "– I followed her, I didn't know where the girls had gone. Greg came out of nowhere. I didn't even know it was him at first. He went to grab Lola. She turned to run away. As soon as she was clear, I took the shot."

He was clearly shaken up, but I could also see his anger building. Why he was angry, I wasn't sure.

"It was only after I shot him I figured out it was him," he exclaimed.

"Okay, thank you Andy. You did the right thing," the flight sergeant tried to reassure him.

His words didn't seem to provide Andy with any comfort; he left his gun on the ground and stormed back to the base.

Flight Sergeant Tanner turned to Lacey and I. "Girls, please go back to the base. It's not safe out here anymore; we need to secure the area and dispose of the body," He told us. His tone was firm, yet I could sense the underlying pain in his voice, he was trying so hard to mask.

Lacey and I headed back to the base. There was no sign of Duckface or Andy, so we went back to check the plane.

The Professor had stopped us before we stepped into the plane.

"What happened? Is everyone all right?" he asked us. I had barely spoken to him lately. No one had. He had wrapped himself up in his work, constantly conducting tests on the samples he had been given. He never shared his findings with us. Whenever I asked, the majority of his responses went straight over my head.

"Greg's dead," I told him.

He smiled as he looked at me and shook his head. "I know that dear, I mean what happened just then," he asked, reiterating his first question.

"Greg's dead... again," Lacey responded wittily.

I couldn't help but laugh. I know it was sick. It was a horrible thing to happen, but the way she said it just set me off. The Professor, just realising what happened, started to chuckle. It didn't take long for us all to be in stitches.

"Why are we laughing?" Lacey asked, trying to calm herself.

The Professor carried on laughing. He had a deep belly laugh, but it was mixed in with the famous Jimmy Carr laugh we all know and love.

The sound of his laugh made me crease up even more.

"Well... at first I was laughing at you... now... I'm laughing at him," I said between gasps. I hadn't laughed this hard in a long time. We were all wiping our eyes as tears ran down our faces.

Once we had all calmed down, we told the Professor what we had just witnessed.

"Oh dear. That isn't good news at all. I'm starting to regret my earlier outburst. This isn't a laughing matter at all," he said firmly.

He hurried outside, mumbling something about needing fresh samples and isolating the virus. We shrugged and carried on into the plane.

As soon as we got into the plane and after hearing our voices, Duckface made her way down.

"Can I talk to you for a minute?" she asked me.

I looked at Lacey, not too sure what she wanted. Lacey shrugged her shoulders. "I'll leave you guys to it, then," she said as she got up and made her way outside.

I smiled at her as she left, before I turned to face Lola. "What is it?" I asked curiously. We barely spoke anymore. She had shrugged me off like she had the rest of the group.

She was hardly pleasant to be around. She wasn't blind or stupid. She knew we didn't have much of a friendship anymore. In fact our freindship was over a long time ago.

"I want to talk to you about Andy," she told me. She seemed to be in a much better mood than she had been previously.

"I think he still likes me, he followed me out and he saved my life," she started. I looked away from her and rolled my eyes. Here we go again. I've endured countless conversations like this with her in the past. She overanalysed everything.

She didn't stop there. "I wouldn't take him back straight away, he has to work to get me back. He obviously likes me though, otherwise why would he follow me out? You know. He's probably realised how much he needs me," she said, confidently.

Oh God, I didn't want to get involved. I don't know why he followed her, he said he came to look for Lacey and I as we had vanished. He probably did. I could see that Andy had tried to keep himself to himself, but damned if I knew if it had anything to do with Duckface or not.

"I don't know why he followed you out, like he said Lacey and I disappeared, so he said he went to look for us. It's anyone's guess. He hasn't spoken to anyone very much, so I can't offer any suggestions." I tried to kill the conversation. I didn't have the energy to sit analysing every single move he made. My mind was still on Greg. I was starting to wonder, how did he even get in?

"Well, if he hasn't spoken to anyone, it must be because he regrets breaking up with me, don't you think?" she asked me; she wasn't going to let this drop.

"I don't know Lola, if you want my advice, don't read too much into it. It was good he was there when he was, he saved your life. If you're that bothered just go and speak to him. Maybe even start by saying thank you," I told her.

She sat thinking for a few minutes. "Yeah, I could say thank you, but I don't want him to think I'm bothered. I still haven't forgiven him. I don't want him to have all the power; I want to be the one to click my fingers and for him to come running."

I groaned. Typical Duckface behaviour. No matter what the poor guy did, she wanted to make him miserable; I hoped he wasn't thinking of reconciling with her. She still wasn't worth the effort.

"Lola, you really need to get a grip. I'm not being funny, but he saved your life. If he wasn't there, chances are you would be dead by now. Give the guy a break. If he wants to get back with you, work it out together. I'm sorry, but that's all I can say to help you," I snapped at her. I didn't mean to be so blunt, but she needed to get a hold of herself.

"Okay, I'll speak to him... Thanks," she replied weakly. She seemed a bit deflated, but I couldn't bear to listen her incessant rambling anymore. My patience with her was already wearing extremely thin. The way her egotistical mind worked was completely baffling to me.

With that, she wandered off. No doubt to find Andy. I sat there shaking my head. I hoped to God he wasn't going to take her back. I felt bad for the guy; he had already endured years with her, and I didn't blame him at all for having enough of it.

Lacey wandered back into the plane shortly after Duckface left.

"What was all that about?" she asked, taking a seat on the sofa.

"You don't want to know," I replied rolling my eyes. The conversation soon reverted back to normal. Or at least what could be classed as normal for us. As we talked, as normal girls do, all the usual subjects came up. Clothes, shoes, funny youtube videos, to name a few.

My mind wandered back to The Corporal. Ryan, as he'd asked me to call him. I wanted to tell Lacey about it. I wanted her perspective on the situation. I needed her advice. At the same time, I didn't want her to think less of me. She was my best and closest friend. I sighed and started the conversation.

"Lace, there's something I want to talk to you about... it's about the Corporal." I started.

She smiled at me. It was a smug *I know what you are going to say* smile. "I know, I've seen the way he looks at you." she told me. "He hasn't been inappropriate with you has he?" She asked me lowering her tone.

"No, nothing like that! He just..." I didn't know what to say. Maybe I was just afraid to admit it to her.

"You like him don't you?" Lacey whispered. Damn, this girl was psychic. I nodded. I couldn't deny it. "I'm not in love with him, I love Nick, I know I do. There's just something about Ryan..." I trailed off.

"I get it, I really do. He's gorgeous. If you were single I'd say go for it. But you're not. And Nick loves you. Just promise me you won't do something you'll regret later." She said.

I smiled and grabbed her hand. "Don't worry, I have no plans to do anything of the sort. In all honesty I just want to make these feelings go away." I told her firmly.

Lacey nodded. "I won't say anything. Just try to keep your distance. I know it's hard given the circumstances, but it's all I can suggest."

I completely agreed. I felt much better after talking it out with Lacey. After all, that was what friends are for.

"Speaking of distance," I started. "Where's everybody else?" I asked.

Chapter 16

Where's Andy?

It wasn't long before Lacey and I had gone looking for the boys. They were taking ages, and I was eager to find out what happened to Greg. I figured they would be able to shed some light on the earlier events.

"Where are they?" Lacey asked me as we stepped outside. We looked all around us; we couldn't see a single soul. The fencing looked completely untouched, as it always had been.

"I have no idea. They must have gone inside," I told her, making my way to Hangar 3.

She followed, keeping up the same pace as me. "Where do you think he got in from?" she asked as I found myself asking myself the same question.

"I don't know hun, don't think he came in through the fence though, when we came out it was all still intact." I was as confused as she was.

"Let's find the rest of them and see if they've found anything," she suggested.

We walked through the entrance door; we couldn't hear anyone moving about inside, so we went to investigate.

We checked the main hall first. Everything was how we left it. The beds were still set up; nothing looked out of the ordinary, so we made our way back to the supply room.

"I bet they've gone into the tunnel," I speculated as the trapdoor was wide open. They obviously weren't in the room; we wandered round anyway and checked around the shelving, just to make sure.

We both leaned over the hole in the floor, the opening to the tunnel. After the rat fiasco, neither of us were in any rush to go back down there. We knew they were down there, and I could see a faint light moving around the bottom.

"Paul, Nick, are you down there?" Lacey shouted down.

We could hear movement, but no one responded. We shone our torches downwards, trying to get a closer look.

The corporal quickly came into view, shielding his eyes from the light.

"We're all down here, girls!" he shouted up to us. "Don't worry we're all okay but don't come down. We're just making sure it's safe." He dismissed us, "Go back to the base, we'll be up shortly." He walked out of sight, obviously carrying on with the search. He was already starting to look a little less attractive.

"Do you think Greg came up from there?" Lacey asked me, slightly concerned.

"I don't know. Your guess is as good as mine," I answered. I was starting to get worried. Maybe we were in more danger than we thought. What if the infected had made their way into the tunnel system? We didn't know for certain, but it certainly brought up more questions we simply couldn't answer.

George was down there with the others. He knew his way around, only he knew where all the exits led out to. I was now 100% certain I had seen Greg alive in his infected state, days after he fell to his untimely death. There's no way he could have gone out the base, yet I was even more mystified as to how he had managed to stay hidden for so long. If there were a tunnel exit somewhere on the base, which there very well could be, it could explain how Greg got to us on the inside.

Even more worrying: in order to do that, he must have kept himself sustained in some way. How did he do it? Although there were many buildings scattered around the base, we certainly hadn't checked them all. Had there been other survivors who hadn't been as lucky as us? Had their safe house been comprised by the infected, including Greg? Were there more of them lurking around? I was full of questions.

"Shall we go back?" Lacey asked me, interrupting my chilling thought process.

"Yeah, let's make a move," I replied, my mind still working overtime.

As we walked out into the daylight, I scanned the area around me. There were no signs of life; everything was quiet. I could still make out faded bloodstains across the tarmac; most had been washed away by the rain. They were ghastly reminders of the battles we had previously faced, taking out our targets from the roof.

There was hardly ever anyone on watch nowadays. We kept the fencing up as an extra precaution, but there was no longer need to place anyone on watch. I had begged to differ.

"Shall we go up to the roof?" I asked Lacey, halfway through my daydream.

"Can do, why?" she asked.

"The infected are coming in from somewhere, although they could be getting into the tunnel system, I think we should still keep an eye out," I replied.

She nodded in agreement. We went back to the base to find our old rifles, then we made our way to the roof.

I hadn't set foot on the roof since the day Greg died – well the first time that Greg died. It felt strange going back up there.

I looked towards the spot he fell from, my mind replaying the events that followed. My eyes cast towards the fire burning in the distance. The flight sergeant had burnt Greg's body; it was the only option, and it was safest all round. Too bad we didn't think of it the first time round.

I looked back to Greg's first resting spot. I couldn't bring myself to look over the edge. I knew he wasn't there, but I still couldn't muster the courage to look down, afraid of what I might see.

My fear of heights had all but vanished. I no longer got the sinking feeling that pulled my heart into my stomach. I always stayed a couple of feet away from the edge, only daring to get closer whilst lying down. Don't get me wrong, I could never sit on the edge with my feet dangling down, that was just a step too far.

It didn't take me long to settle into my previously familiar surroundings. I took the rifle and scope from my back and placed it on the roof, scoping towards Hangar 3. Lacey had set up next to me and was checking the areas outside of the fencing zones.

I stayed clear of the area around the fire. My mind was already getting the better of me, and I didn't want to dwell on it. Greg was a good man; he was finally at peace.

I looked towards the side nearest the woods, but even with my magnifying scope, I couldn't see into the trees. I wondered whether the infected were in there. I couldn't see any movement, only the wind bristling through the last of the remaining leaves. It was cold outside; my hands were already starting to lose their feeling. I sniffled as the cold attacked my sinuses.

I pulled my scope back towards the entrance to Hangar 3. I could see the boys making their way out the building. They looked tired. They obviously hadn't found anything of interest. I wondered if they had seen the same monster-sized rats we did? They would have, of course, handled it a lot better than we did. I couldn't imagine any of them screaming and running away.

I quickly pulled my scope up as I noticed something out of the ordinary up on the roof of Hangar 3. It was only a small-single story building. It was the height of a bungalow, our main base towered over the smaller building laid out in front of us.

I was amazed it had taken me so long to spot. There on the roof was a darkened stain. I angled my scope for a closer look;

the boys had spotted Lacey and I and were trying to wave to us. Lacey waved back, but I ignored them and kept my attention on the roof.

The closer I looked, the more the stain came into view. As the clouds cleared letting more sunlight through, I could see the colour more clearly. It was blood. I looked around the roof in more detail and noticed more speckles of blood, lining the roof below.

I looked closer at the speckles which had formed on the roof when I noticed... they were handprints.

I had solved the mystery as to how Greg had got in. He must have climbed onto the roof somehow and dropped down inside the fencing. He must have seen Lola coming and dropped down to attack. Luckily (or unluckily depending on how you want to look at it) Andy was there to stop him before he caused any real damage.

I shouted Lacey over; she was already looking at me, bemused as to what I was so fixated on. So I pointed it out to her.

"Oh my God, is that blood?" she asked me. I nodded as she leaned in for a closer look.

"Do you think that's how he got in? He climbed up?" she said, following the exact same thought process I did.

"Pretty much. It makes more sense than him coming up through the tunnel don't you think?" I asked her.

"Definitely," she replied. "We need to tell the others. I don't think they've spotted it yet."

I agreed. "You stay here, hun. I'll go down and grab them. I'll bring them up here so they can see for themselves," I told her.

I made my way downstairs to tell the others what we had seen. Nick stopped me before I had a chance to get to them.

"Are you in a mood or something babe? How come you didn't wave back?" He asked. He looked slightly hurt.

I looked up at him, still eager to gather everyone on the roof. "No, I'm fine, just saw something on the roof. Will you go up? Lacey is up there, she'll show you," I told him, making my way to the others. He stopped me again.

"Why what is it? What have you seen?" he asked, trying to get more information out of me.

"Babe, just go upstairs. I'll be up with the rest in a few minutes," I didn't mean to snap at him, but he was starting to get on my nerves slightly. He did as he was told. I turned to grab the others and show them the marks on the roof.

I raised my voice slightly so they could all hear me. "Can you all come up to the roof please? I've got something I want to show you all."

They all turned around and looked at me. Leon was the first to respond. "If you're taking us all up to the roof to show us your boobs, you can save yourself the effort and flash us right here," he joked. I ignored him; it was typical Leon he was always making jokes. Underneath his pervy exterior, he was a nice guy. I didn't bite back. Instead, I put it down to male stupidity and carried on.

"I know how Greg got in!" I exclaimed. That was all I needed to say, without another word they all made their way upstairs, no questions asked.

I was greeted on the roof by Nick; I could tell he now understood my urgency as he helped me up onto the roof. As everyone else clambered up he pulled me into his arms. "I'm sorry babe I was just worried, thought I had done something wrong."

I stood on my tiptoes and kissed him. "It's fine, sorry I snapped. Just needed to tell everyone so we could stop it before anymore came up" I replied. We had a good relationship. Even when spending this much time together, it didn't harm our relationship. We were always honest and straight with each other. We always worked through our problems. I had never been in such a strong relationship before. It's why I didn't hesitate to say yes, when he had asked me to marry him. The more I thought back to our history together, the more feelings I had towards him. Ryan was soon becoming a distant memory.

I felt sad as I thought back to all our wedding plans. We were going to get married in the summer, next year. It never really hit me until now, that I would never get the wedding I had spent so much time planning and wanting. Although I hadn't bought it yet, I already had the perfect dress in mind. It was a corset-style ivory gown; it was strapless and floated down to the floor so elegantly. It had small Swarovski crystals making their way down the bodice, floating down towards the floor.

The hotel was already booked; it was to take place at Mottram Hall, a grand hotel on the outskirts of Prestbury. We had spent over two years saving for our dream wedding, and although it was still a while off, we were so looking forward to it.

I put my wedding dreams to the back of my mind; it was starting to depress me. I had more important things at hand. One by one, each of the men took it in turns to view the bloodstains on the roof.

"This is incredible," the Professor said amazed. "The upper body strength required to complete such a task, they are indeed showing incredible signs of intelligence beyond what we conceived possible," he babbled on.

"We couldn't find anything out of the ordinary in the tunnels" Paul piped up. "Apart from a couple of rats," he added.

Lacey and I looked at each other. The thought of those rats made us both shudder. We ran away as soon as we saw them, but no one else knew we were down there. We had decided between ourselves to keep it that way.

The flight sergeant addressed us all. "I have been speaking to the Professor here, about the infection in livestock. He has confirmed to me that animals can contain the virus. However, they do not react to it the same as humans do. Although they are not considered dangerous, one bite can cause the same effect as an infected human. Therefore, we will keep the tunnel off limits and for emergency use only."

We all agreed. I would be happy if I never had to set foot in that place again. My two main fears growing up were spiders and rats. To this day I still don't fare too well with either. Infected rats were just a step too far.

Sergeant Tanner continued. "However, there are far more important issues at hand. If the infected, as I suspect, can indeed now climb, we need to increase security to prevent this from happening again," the flight sergeant spoke up. "We need barbed wire across the top of the roof. I suspect this won't stop the infected completely, but it will slow them down."

He was right; we couldn't risk this happening again. What if Duckface and Andy hadn't been there? He could have jumped on top of me or Lacey, or he could have made his way into the tunnel and ambushed us there. We were very lucky to get away. Thank God Andy was there.

I wondered what he and Duckface were talking about; I hadn't seen either of them for a good hour. I didn't have to wait long to find my answer. Duckface poked her head out of the roof hatch.

"Is Andy with you?" she asked peering about.

"No, I thought you went to find him?" I asked.

"I did, I couldn't find him anywhere, so I presumed he was with you. I heard you all on the roof, so I came to check, but he's not here. Obviously," she pointed out snottily.

"Well, he must be around here somewhere," Paul said looking around. "He can't have gone far."

We all made our way downstairs, to try to find him. He looked upset when he walked off, he probably needed some time to calm down, and collect his thoughts.

Chapter 17

Keeping the Peace

We checked every inch of the base; we couldn't find Andy. He had gone. It didn't take us long to realise that, his car had also vanished.

We were starting to panic. Where the hell was he? He was in the outside world completely alone. He had taken his belongings from his room, along with his guns and some ammunition from the store.

The boys quickly hopped into the trucks, formed a search team and headed out. Lacey and I were left in the base with the Professor and Duckface, even George had joined the search party.

"Where the hell could he have gone?" I asked Duckface, who was completely inconsolable.

"I... don't... know," she gasped between sobs.

"Well, did he say anything to you before he left?" I asked, trying to get something out of her.

She shook her head. It was useless; I couldn't get anything rational out of her. Even Lacey was trying to calm her down. We sat her back in the plane, and got her a glass of water.

"Why... has... he... left me?" she cried, I could barely make out what she was saying, she was crying that much.

Lacey looked at me and shook her head. "I'm sure he's fine Lola, the boys will find him, and they'll bring him back," she said, patting her on the back.

Duckface grimaced as she pulled away from her. Lacey stood up "I'm only trying to help, Lola. I'm just as worried as you are," she told her with an irritable tone in her voice. I could see she was trying to stay calm and rational, but she was finding it hard.

"You... d... d... don't care." Duckface gasped for air.

Lacey was about to retaliate as the Professor stepped in. He took Lacey's spot and sat down beside her.

"Now, Lola we haven't always seen eye to eye, but we all have your best interests at heart. You need to stop this, for Andy's sake and try and help us figure out where he could have gone. Can you do that?" he asked.

She shook her head. "Just... leave me alone," she said, deflated. She wailed and started crying all again.

"Okay, we will give you some time to compose yourself. We'll be outside if you want to come and talk to us, won't we girls?" he was speaking to her as if she were a small child. It seemed to be working.

Lacey and I both nodded. There wasn't much else we could do. We obviously weren't going to get anything out of her in this state. We left the plane and went to sit with the Professor.

"I take it neither of you know anything of Andy's whereabouts?" the Professor asked.

I answered him. "No, I haven't got a clue. He's been keeping himself to himself lately; hardly any of us have talked to him."

The Professor was trying to make sense of the situation. "If he was keeping to himself, he may have had this planned for a while."

"What do you mean?" Lacey asked.

"Well, it doesn't sound like he's up and left without a destination in mind. He must have had his reasons," the Professor observed looking up towards the plane. "He's a smart boy, he wouldn't leave unless he were sure of where he was going. He knows the danger, and he knows wandering out into the world would be a fool's game. There is no way he wouldn't have had a heading or a safe place in mind."

The Professor was right. He had been spending most of his time working out and training. He had put a lot more time into it than any of us had, and he was way more advanced as a result. Looking back, it was as if he was preparing for a fight. He must have considered leaving for a while.

"But why wouldn't he tell us?" Lacey asked.

I answered before the Professor had a chance to. "He knew we would try and stop him. This is obviously something he felt he had to do for himself."

The Professor added, "He probably didn't want to put anyone else in danger."

The Professor had a nasty habit of being right. That definitely sounded like Andy; he would rather put himself in danger than risk anyone else. He was always putting others first. But still, it didn't condone his behaviour. Leaving without telling anyone, it just wasn't on.

"I'm going to go check on Lola, and then I'm going to check Andy's room. See if I can find any clues as to why he's disappeared," I told them both.

I made my way back towards the plane, to see if Lola could offer any useful information.

When I pulled back the curtain into the living area, she was sat on the sofa, staring into space.

"Lola, are you okay?" I asked.

She didn't turn to look at me; she just nodded. She carried on staring into space. She had stopped crying; her breathing was almost back to normal. She took in a few deep, fragmented breaths but made no effort to respond.

"Are you ready to talk yet?" I asked, trying to be as nice to her as possible. Again, she shook her head.

"Okay... When you're ready to talk just come and get me. If not I'll come and check on you in a little while." I was doing what the Professor did, and was speaking to her like a child.

She didn't acknowledge me, so I left her alone and made my way over to the next base, where Andy spent most of his time.

As I walked through the fencing area I could see the tyre marks the boys had left as they wheel-spinned their way out of the base in a hurry. I wandered around the base, trying to figure out what Andy was thinking, when he decided to leave us.

I opened the door into his room and sat on his bed. The room was neat and tidy; he had even made his bed before he left. It was an understatement to say I was upset with him.

I understood his reasons up to a point. But to not say anything to anyone, that was just rude. The more I thought about it the angrier I became. My fiancé was now out there, searching for him along with the others. If anything happened to Nick, I would hold him solely responsible.

I searched his whole room from top to bottom. I even checked under the bed, trying to find some clue as to where he had gone. After a while, I had no choice but to give up. I had torn his whole room upside down, and completely drawn a blank.

I wandered into the kitchen; I needed a drink and a few moments to collect my thoughts. I would have loved nothing more than a nice cool glass of white wine to calm my nerves. I hadn't had a drop of alcohol since this whole fiasco began. I felt like a recovering alcoholic of the verge of a relapse.

I was about to pull open the fridge. We had used the powdered orange from the MRE packs to make fruit juice. That would have to do. It was then I saw the envelope hanging from the fridge door.

How on earth did we all miss this? I pulled it off and opened it up. It read:

As you have probably all noticed, I've left the base.

Please don't try to look for me, I've gone to find my family. I know they're out there somewhere, I owe it to them to find them.
Tell Lola I'm sorry.
Don't worry, stay safe. Love to you all.
Andy x

I went to put the note back into the envelope when I felt something hard in the corner. I pulled out Andy's wedding ring.

I guess reconciliation wasn't on the cards after all. He started to go up in my estimations. At least he had left a note. I went back to the main base, to get through to the boys and bring them back, there wasn't any more we could do. Even if they found him, he wouldn't come back. There was no point risking the whole group's safety. He obviously had his heart set.

I rushed back to the base and met with Lacey and the Professor. I showed them the note. The Professor instantly dialled through to the boys from the radio transmitter, whilst Lacey, and I went to have a conversation with Duckface.

We boarded the plane and, with the envelope in hand, we sat beside Duckface. She still hadn't moved.

"Lola, we've found something we need to show you. Andy left a note," I told her.

For the first time she broke her gaze and looked up at me. A tear fell down her face. I handed her the envelope, with the ring still inside.

She read the note and pulled the ring out of the envelope. She broke down again.

"It's okay, we know where he's gone. He's going to find his family, he'll probably bring them back here," Lacey spoke softly, trying again to calm her down. She kept her distance but still tried to rationalise with her, and stay positive.

"No, he won't," she sobbed. "I know he won't."

"How do you know he won't, Lola?" I asked. I didn't like the way she said she knew he wouldn't. She knew more than she was letting on. I needed to get the truth out of her.

She didn't say anything. I looked questioningly at Lacey. "Lola. Did you speak to Andy before he left?" I asked firmly.

She carried on sobbing. Lacey was starting to see where I was going with this. "Lola, if you have any feelings for Andy or care at all for his well-being, I think for his sake you should tell us," she pushed.

She looked up at us. "He told me it was over... that there was no chance of us ever being anything... he said I changed, and I wasn't the same." She started to cry again.

I knew exactly what he meant. She had turned into a selfish, tantrum throwing, two-faced, stuck-up cow.

"Did he tell you he was leaving?" I asked, now slightly irritated. She nodded. "He said it... it wasn't healthy being trapped here together..."

Lacey interrupted before I could get a word in edgeways. She was not at all pleased. "So you knew Andy was leaving? But you didn't say anything. You lied to us and said you didn't know. You watched as everyone left to search for him, when you knew where he was going all along?" Lacey was fuming.

"I'm sorry your relationship didn't work out and all that, but that was your own damned fault. You risked the lives of my husband, her fiancé and the rest of the group. Because you were too damn selfish to say anything!" she carried on.

Duckface reared her head; her grief had turned to anger. I saw the hatred in her eyes as she glared at Lacey. "You don't know anything. I don't even know where his family live. For your information, he didn't have anything to do with them when we were together," she told Lacey.

"And I wonder why that is. Is it because his family saw straight through you and knew what a selfish little cow you really are?" Lacey wasn't holding back. She had wanted to say something to Duckface for a long time. Lacey had finally cracked.

I tried to calm the situation down. "That's enough both of you. This isn't helping matters at all. There's nothing we can do about it—"

"Me, selfish? That's rich coming from you. You have no right to question my relationship. It's my husband and my life; it's no concern of yours!" Duckface cut me off mid-sentence.

"In case you haven't noticed, it's all of our concern. Grow up and take a long hard look at yourself," Lacey hit back. "You're just a good for nothing, whiny little bitch. No wonder he left you."

Duckface snapped. She slapped Lacey right across the face. I stood wide-mouthed as it happened. I couldn't believe what I was seeing. I knew they hated each other with a passion, but

I could never have foreseen this. Duckface was always all talk; I had never seen her lash out at anyone.

Lacey turned to Lola and grinned. "I've been waiting for you to do that for so long." With that, she grabbed Duckface by the neck and dragged her outside. She threw her down the last couple of stairs as I ran after them.

They both snapped. Duckface launched herself at Lacey as Lacey swiftly dodged out the way. Duckface fell to the floor. The boys had just pulled in at that moment; all were as wide-eyed as myself and the Professor, who had rushed over to see what all the commotion was about.

"You stupid cow!" Duckface spat. "I always knew you were beneath me!"

She lunged at Lacey as she side stepped and pushed her back. Duckface was going ballistic; she kept running at Lacey as Lacey simply dodged her attacks. She didn't even retaliate or fight back. What was going on?

Duckface made one last attempt, grazing her nail down Lacey's left cheek. She drew blood. That was Lacey's turning point. She punched her square in the face. Duckface fell to the floor instantly.

The flight sergeant ran over at this point. "Girls what on earth do you think you're doing? Back to your living quarters immediately!" he yelled. He was furious; I had never seen the Tanner so angry. His voice shook throughout the whole of the hangar.

Duckface pulled herself up from the floor. "Fuck you all, you're all dead to me!" she snarled as she made her way back to the plane. She had completely lost it.

Paul and Nick ran over to us. "What was all that about?" Nick asked.

"It's a long story, I'll you about it later," I told him. I watched as both girls went their separate ways.

The flight sergeant, still outraged ordered us all to our living quarters. "I want all of you to get to bed. It's late, and I have had enough of these childish antics for one day!" He scorned us like we were all naughty children. After the drama of today, I couldn't blame him.

Chapter 18

Hostile Takeover

We were awoken the next morning by the Corporal Jameson frantically banging on the doors.

"Everyone get up quickly, there's been a breach."

I rolled over and checked the clock on our makeshift bedside table, five thirty-four a.m. I groaned. I pulled the covers back and shook Nick to wake up.

"What's the matter baby?" he grumbled, still half asleep.

"Think the corporal wants to start training early," I mumbled, pulling my clothes on, making no attempt to get out of bed.

"EVERYONE TO THE BASE NOW! THE INFECTED ARE EVERYWHERE!" the corporal screamed.

I could hear gunshots coming from the main base. "Shit, let's go!" I pulled at Nick, who was already practically dressed. We were wide awake now.

We ran towards the base. The corporal was right. The infected were everywhere. What the hell was going on? There were hundreds of them! They had made their way to the fence and were violently shaking the barrier, trying to get to us. We picked up our pace; we were full on sprinting down the narrow passageway whilst the corporal was holding open the door, motioning us through. His eyes locked with mine as I ran.

George was positioned on the roof; he was taking out as many as he could. We were completely overrun. For every infected George took out, ten more appeared in its place.

I couldn't believe this was happening, how did they even get in? Apart from Greg, we hadn't seen any of the infected anywhere on the base for weeks now.

We rushed through the door as the Corporal Jameson swiftly slammed it shut behind us. Bangs echoed all around us as the infected launched themselves at the shutters and swarmed around our building. They knew we were inside, and they wouldn't stop until they got in. They were relentless.

The flight sergeant did a quick headcount, making sure we were all accounted for.

"What's going on? How did they get in?" I asked the group. I was so scared. I had never seen this many of them in one place. There was no escape. I trembled as I heard them screech. They had an immense desperation to get to us. They were fast, and their strength was building. I could tell by the heavy thuds echoing throughout the room.

I looked around each individual in the group; someone was missing. I knew George was on the roof; I saw him on my way towards the base. But where was Duckface?

Lacey saw me looking around the room, she answered for me. "She's gone," she answered simply.

"What do you mean she's gone?" I demanded.

"Well, there's no sign of her anywhere and your car's gone, too," Lacey told me.

I couldn't believe it. She just left. And the stupid bitch had the audacity to take my car.

George made his way down from the roof. "There's too many of them. We can fight them off for a while, but more of them keep coming. The main gate's been left open. Flight Sergeant, the lock down on the main base has been compromised. That's where they're coming from."

The flight sergeant looked confused. "That can't be, only I have the code. It's kept in my office desk. Besides, why would anyone want to do that?"

I had my suspicions. But we had more important issues at hand. We had our base on lockdown. But we weren't prepared for an attack of this magnitude.

"Everyone to the roof. Take as much ammunition as you can carry. We'll fight off as many as we can, now" Tanner ordered.

We all ran through to the ammunition store; the Sergeant quickly typed in the code. We pulled out as many guns as possible.

The thuds echoing around the room got louder and louder as more of the infected descended on us.

We threw the ammunition onto the roof. I pulled myself up on the roof, ready for battle. The sight before me made me shudder. Thousands of the undead surged towards us. There was no way we could kill them all; we didn't have enough ammo. Even if we took each one out with a head shot, we would still be running extremely low.

The stench of that many corpses huddled together was overpowering. Death filled the air. I was frozen on the spot. The fear took over. My mind was shutting down. I knew what I needed to do, but getting my body to do it was a completely different matter. Everyone around me was busy setting up, readying themselves for action.

I couldn't move. I wasn't helping matters; I was just staring into the foul-smelling, rotting, infection-wielding crowd beneath us. They were like animals; they only had basic primal instincts. They wanted to feed. They felt no pain, no emotion and no fear. They were hunters, and we were the hunted.

I was blocking everything out around me; I didn't mean to, I had just shut myself down. Nick quickly snapped me out of it. He saw me staring into the distance, and he knew something wasn't right. He shook me until I came back to reality.

"Babe, come on, we need you, snap out of it!" he said as he pulled me close.

After a few minutes, I came around. My eyes came into focus as I stared into his eyes. I was back.

From behind Nick I saw the Corporal Jameson and Leon launching grenades into the crowd. Explosions were going off all around us. Body parts flew through the air, dispersing through the crowd.

The infected were still overpowering us. Although the explosion cut through the crowd, as soon as the smoke cleared, more had taken their place.

The infected didn't seem at all bothered about the danger from the gunfire or explosives. They didn't even turn their heads or acknowledge their fallen comrades. The only goal they had was to feed on us, and succumb us to the same virus that had infected them.

Damned if I was going to end up like that. I grabbed hold of my rifle and aimed it directly below. I was targeting the infected closest to the building. They were much easier to take out, given that they were packed in so tightly together, like a tin of sardines.

The infected closest to us started to fall. I was aiming for the head, the force from the bullets sent the heads of my targets flying. It was like watching a watermelon explode. Viscous bodily fluids splattered more of the viral hosts. They simply cast the dead bodies to one side and stepped over them in a desperate attempt to gain entry.

This carried on for hours. The bodies of men, women and even children were starting to pile up around the base. The children were by far the most disturbing. They ran with such speed and agility, their screams were far higher pitched than those of the adults. They had the same drive as the rest, propelling them forward. They climbed over the adults to get closer to the front. They were small and nimble, they used their strengths to their advantage. Although they resembled the height and features of a child, their whole demeanour was far more terrifying. They were predators, just like the rest.

I watched one small girl, no older than six or seven clamber her way through the crowd. I was fixated on her for a few seconds, watching her through my scope. Her mouth was covered in fresh blood; her mouth was open, as more blood pooled down to her blue teddy bear print T-shirt. Her arms were flailing wildly, she was desperate to get to the front of the crowd. She crawled her way to the front and looked straight up at me. Her skin was deathly pale. Her hollow eyes bore into me as she snarled up, her face creased into a look of pure evil as she gnashed out at the air.

She jumped, a lot further than I thought possible and attempted to climb the building. I put a bullet through her head before she had a chance to get any further.

I turned my attention to the rest of the crowd. The sound of the gunshots and explosives going off all around me was deafening, I could barely hear myself think.

The flight sergeant was screaming something at us, but I couldn't hear him over the noise. My ears were starting to ring from the blasts, whilst my head was throbbing.

The corporal was pointing down. We called a ceasefire, as we ran over to see what it was the corporal was pointing at.

The shutters were starting to cave in. They weren't built to handle the weight that was now pushing against them. I could hear the metal straining as the crowd pushed its way forward.

We had to do something. I thought back to the incident with the fence. We had already killed countless infected on the roof, but it wasn't enough. Innards were strewn all over the base, staining the walls and the floor. The overpowering stench was getting a lot worse, and we were running out of ammo.

It was only a matter of time before the infected forced their way in. We were safe enough on the roof for the time being, but it wasn't a long-term solution. We had no food or water, and our ammunition was low.

"It's no use, save your ammo. Stop shooting"!" Flight Sergeant Tanner ordered; I could tell he was deflated.

We were fighting a losing battle. We had nowhere to run. There was no way out; we could all fit in the trucks, but without a clear path, it was useless. We would be lucky if we lasted a few minutes out there.

We could stay on the roof. But without food or water, we wouldn't last very long.

I held onto Nick. At that moment, I was waiting to die. All hope was lost.

"What do we do now, Flight Sergeant?" Leon asked solemnly.

"I am honoured to have fought next to each and every one of you. You have all shown such willingness. For that, I am grateful, but I'm afraid our battle has been lost. We can carry on fighting, but I fear that would be a fool's errand. We've been greatly overpowered. Our only viable option would be to retreat," the flight sergeant addressed us all.

We all agreed. "How exactly are we going to retreat?" I asked, "We have nowhere to go." The group around me nodded. George answered me.

"We get into the tunnel system, it's our only chance of escape," he replied matter-of-fact.

I looked towards Hangar 3. I could barely see the building; the infected had torn down the gate and were already climbing onto the roof. There was no chance we could make it to the building alive, without being bitten or scratched. The small gleam of hope I held onto was vastly deteriorating.

"And how exactly are we going to get past them?" Paul asked.

George chuckled. "That isn't the only entrance, you know."

We all looked around at him, what was he trying to say?

We didn't have time to stand around and chat – at that moment we heard an almighty clunk. The shutters had started to give way. If we were going to escape, it was now or never.

We scrambled down from the roof as George led the way to the second tunnel entrance, which just happened to be within the base.

He guided us to the plane and headed towards the wheels. He lifted the trap door and, to our surprise, there was another entrance. I couldn't believe it, in all my time at the base I had never noticed it.

He hurried us all down. The Professor went down first, as soon as he got to the bottom he called up, to let us know he was okay.

Lacey made her way down next, followed by George. He had armed us all with flashlights beforehand. I was about to make my way down next when the shutter gave way once more. It had created a small opening, a space big enough for the infected to get through.

The flight sergeant started to lay down some covering fire. "Everyone in the tunnel NOW!" he shouted as three of the infected made their way through. They were all dressed in military uniforms as they sprinted their way towards us. The flight sergeant, Leon and the corporal quickly dispatched of them.

Josh grabbed my arm and pulled me back. "You need to get down there now!" he urged. I had my gun ready; I wasn't going anywhere without Nick.

Nick and Paul had run off to help the flight sergeant. I shouted for them to come back. The opening in the shutters was starting to open further. Flight sergeant Tanner ran to the truck.

I knew what he was doing, whilst the boys fired at the infected he was going to block our path with the truck. I was halfway down the ladders at this point.

I stopped, pleading for the boys to hurry. They couldn't hear me over the gunfire. The infected were getting closer; the boys were within arm's length of them now. They carried on shooting, clinging to their training for dear life, one half covering the other as they fell back.

By this point, the flight sergeant was in the truck, running over the infected as he made his way to the shutters. There were at least ten of them on the inside with us, and they kept pouring out.

The corporal grimaced as he shot a small boy. I pulled my handgun up, ready to provide them with covering fire.

I was too late. As Nick and Paul were backing up, one of the infected grasped onto Josh. Leon rushed over to help, but he was a few seconds too late.

The infected former soldier bit down on Josh's neck as others, sensing the fresh blood that had been spilled, changed direction heading straight towards their new victim.

Josh screamed in pain as they ripped through his flesh, tearing him limb from limb. Blood covered the once white concrete floor as, finally, he stopped fighting.

Leon dispatched of the whole group in one fell swoop. I could see the pain in his eyes as he lost his brother in arms.

The flight sergeant had managed to block the entrance with the truck. With the area secure for the moment, I made my way down.

The boys headed towards the trapdoor. Paul successfully made his way down along with the Nick. Corporal Jameson was running towards the trapdoor as Tanner was getting out of the truck.

I heard the sound of the glass smash in the truck as the infected pushed their way through. The corporal screamed for the flight sergeant as the newly reanimated Josh ran towards him. Yet Tanner was trapped; the horde on the outside had almost made their way in. He tried to fight off Josh, but he had lost his gun in the scuffle.

The corporal was about to make his way out as the flight sergeant shouted back. "STOP! Don't you dare, get into that tunnel and close the door."

He was still struggling with Josh. He was trapped between the passenger seat and the door. "GO NOW!" he screamed as the horde behind him found their grasp on the flight sergeant.

With that the corporal slammed the trapdoor shut, and turned to face us all.

We were all stood in the pitch black, with only our torches to light the way. I was clinging onto Nick. I thought I was going to lose him. I couldn't bear seeing him so close to the infected. He could have easily been in Josh's shoes right now. Poor Josh, seeing him getting ripped apart, hearing him scream and writhe in pain. That would haunt me for a long time.

Chapter 19

Isles Woods

"What do we do now?" Paul asked, looking to the corporal.

He shook his head, not quite knowing what to say, he was still in shock. He had just lost his mentor. I knew how he felt. We all looked to Tanner for guidance. He acted like a father figure to me, without him I felt lost.

He was a great man. He lived for others. His main goal in life was to save as many survivors as he could. He wanted to build a better future. His final gift to us saved us all. He forfeited his life, to save ours. I vowed to myself I would never forget that, his final act of selflessness.

We heard a crash from above. The shutter must have completely caved through as we heard masses of footsteps directly above us. We needed to get away, fast.

We all stayed silent as George led us down a small dark passageway, much narrower than the last.

"We need to get to Hangar 3," he whispered. "There are emergency backpacks in the supply room."

"How do we know it's safe?" Nick whispered back.

"We don't, but it's a risk we need to take," the corporal answered, his voice barely audible.

We could still hear the infected trampling above us, but the further away from the base we got, the quieter it became. That was a good sign.

It didn't take us long to reach the end of the narrow corridor. Our surroundings were starting to look a lot more familiar as we came upon the main passageway. I thought back to the rats that had caused our swift getaway last time, I squeezed Nick's hand even tighter. I was more aware of the floor around me, I knew how big those things were, and I certainly wasn't going to let any of them near me.

George took us to the wooden ladders, which led out into the supply room. The corporal was the first to climb the ladders. He stopped halfway up trying to listen out for any movement coming from above.

The coast was clear. The corporal slowly and carefully opened the trapdoor. We had to stay as quiet as possible. He peered out before looking back to us and nodding. Leon followed shortly behind.

They started throwing down the emergency backpacks. Nick and Paul started to hand them out at the bottom.

After the third bag came down we heard a thump on the supply room door. The corporal and Leon both turned around.

There, in the small window, they saw one of the infected throwing himself at the door. It was another former military man. He was riddled with signs of infection. He screeched a sound I never thought humanly possible as he used his whole body as a battering ram.

We heard similar screeching in the distance. He had alerted the others. Our cover was blown. Within seconds more and more piled in front of the door, trying desperately to find a way in.

Leon quickly threw some boxes of ammunition down along with a few extra handguns.

"We need to get out of here before we attract any more attention, let's just take the rest of these bags and go," the corporal ordered.

"But what about the...?" Leon tried to ask. He got cut short.

"No, we haven't got any time. I'm not losing anyone else." He threw the remaining backpacks inside, along with Nick's fishing gear as Leon made his way down.

With one swift move, the corporal pulled the handle clean off the trapdoor. As soon as he was inside he slammed the door shut.

Seconds later the all-too-familiar sound of a door being broken through could be heard from above.

"Quick, pass me that rope," the corporal whispered to Leon. He was pointing to one of the backpacks. Leon swiftly passed it up to the Corporal.

The infected were getting smarter. They had seen where we had escaped from and were scratching at the trapdoor and the floor around us. The corporal flicked the latch into place and wrapped the rope around the ladder.

"That should hold them back for a while," he said as he tied the final knot.

"I suggest we make an immediate exit," the Professor advised.

I wasn't about to argue. We all pulled on our heavy backpacks. "Christ, what on earth is in here?" I whispered. I looked over to Nick; he was busy getting his fishing gear in order.

I rolled my eyes. Typical. We needed a quick getaway, and he refused to let go of his prized possessions.

We followed George down the long winding passageway. The smell was certainly more pleasant down here than it was up there.

The further into the tunnel system we went, the more my eyes adjusted to the darkness. The area all around us was filled with damp. The weather hadn't been kind to us, lately.

Water fell from the ceiling forming small puddles down the centre of our path.

"George, where are we going?" I asked after we had been walking for a while.

"We're nearly there, don't worry," came George's simple reply.

"Where is there?" Lacey asked, slightly annoyed. She was starting to get agitated. We all were. We had lost everything. Even more importantly, had lost two of our own. We had narrowly escaped from the infected, and our base was now completely overrun.

"Isles Woods of course," George exclaimed, as if we should have known.

I stopped. "Why are we going into the woods?" I asked.

It was the corporal's turn to respond. "It's the only exit out of the base."

"Okay, let's just get there, I'm exhausted," I moaned. That day took everything out of me. Now that the adrenaline had worn off, my body had started to ache all over. My head was starting to pound; the effects from the dehydration and my shoulder was throbbing where, yet again, I had been feeling the effects of the kickback from my rifle.

We traipsed deeper into the tunnel; the puddles started to get bigger and bigger as we went along. My feet were starting to hurt.

"I don't know how much further I can carry on" I groaned. "My feet are killing me, my head's banging and this backpack is too heavy."

It was taking its toll on Lacey as well. "This is carrying on forever, guys," she moaned.

"There's an opening just up ahead," George pointed out. "Can you feel that breeze? It's the fresh air coming through."

He led us down a narrow passage. I could see a faint light creeping out from the end of the tunnel.

"Finally," I huffed. I stopped as I neared the end, slowing down my pace. It was indeed an exit into the woods. But it had caved in. Only a small, muddy crawlspace could be seen at the top of the opening, leading out into the daylight.

Great. Just what I wanted to see. Nothing was straightforward. We threw our bags down as I sat on the floor near the exit.

"I don't suppose there's another exit somewhere?" I asked, trying to be optimistic.

"I'm sorry this is the only one," George told us. "I had no idea it had caved in. Saying that, I haven't been here for years."

Well, he failed to mention that when we started our little journey. But we had no option. Nick and Paul went over to the opening and pulled some of the mud and debris back.

"We can all fit through there, it's fine!" Paul said.

Lacey glared at him. I joined in with the staring contest. We had no extra clothes, no hot shower waiting for us. We would get covered in dirt and grime and God knows what was on the other side of that wall.

As we all sat there, contemplating our next move. The familiar rustling sound could be heard in the distance. Eugh, rats! I had almost forgotten they were there. I hadn't seen them along our journey; they must have been startled by the new people taking over their home.

I suppose that was a good enough excuse as any to get moving. Leon was the first to try it out. He pulled himself up and crawled through the small space. As soon as he was out Nick handed him his backpack.

"All clear!" he shouted back to us.

Lacey and I stayed towards the back, we figured the boys could widen the opening for us, leaving more space for us to push through.

I felt sorry for the Professor; his stereotypical white lab coat was going to be ruined after this. It was already showing signs of wear from our earlier ordeal.

Finally, it was our turn. The surge of rats coming towards us certainly made us pick up our pace. We scrambled towards our small exit and pushed ourselves through. I looked back to the corporal, who was the last one out.

Rats flowed towards him like a wave crashing down. There were hundreds of them, what were they running from?

It didn't take me long to find the answer. The corporal's torchlight made its way down the long dark passageway we had just come from.

There, in front of us, limping towards us was the flight sergeant.

He was all banged up; he looked as if he had just come out of a bar fight. Blood trickled down from his forehead as he struggled towards us.

The rats beneath us were going mental, they were swirling all around the corporal's feet, trying to get away. The corporal tried to make his way forward wading through the army of rats.

"Flight Sergeant, is that you? Are you okay?" the Corporal shouted.

The flight sergeant pulled his head up slowly. He looked quizzically at the corporal. He bared his teeth and let out an almighty screech.

He was infected. He sprinted towards Corporal Jameson as the Corporal Jameson scrambled over the rats, trying to get out. He pulled himself up into the crawlspace and made his way through.

The flight sergeant grabbed onto his boot as we all tried to pull the corporal out.

The corporal managed to kick his way free as we all fell into a pile at the bottom of the opening.

The flight sergeant was now halfway through the opening.

We scrambled trying to get up as he snarled hungrily.

From out of nowhere, George stood at the top of the opening and smashed down a large, heavy rock straight onto the flight sergeant's head.

He instantly went limp. We heard the crunch as his skull caved in. Blood seeped through from under the rock, trailing down the opening.

The corporal fell to his knees and sobbed. I had never thought it possible. The corporal was as strong willed as the flight sergeant was. But he was broken. We all were. We had lost so much in such a short space of time.

I looked around each person. Signs of exhaustion were present, along with fear, uncertainty and sadness.

We no longer had the security of the base. Our leader was dead, along with Josh, one of our protectors.

Andy had vanished along with Duckface.

I thought of Duckface, and I scowled. She had betrayed us all. There was no doubt in my mind that she had unlocked the main base, and set the horde of undead hurtling towards our safe house. She would have done it out of spite.

She knew Andy wouldn't have her if she were the last woman on earth, so she seemed determined to make that happen.

I had no idea where either of them had gone. But I hoped to God she was still alive. If I ever saw her again, I'd kill her myself. First off, for setting the infected free, secondly for stealing my car. More importantly, for murdering Tanner and Josh. I was holding her completely and utterly responsible. Had she not opened the main base or left the gate wide open, we wouldn't be in this mess. She was the most vindictive, evil, heartless bitch I had ever laid eyes on. And I vowed to myself I'd make sure she got what was coming to her. Whatever the cost.

I looked around my new surroundings. We were in the middle of the woods. Leaves lined the floor around us as mud and water pushed through from the woodland floor. The mud was thick, with every step I took it tried to consume me, pulling my feet further to the floor.

I started to shiver, it was freezing. Although the trees provided some shelter, the chilling breeze was still able to cut through the trees blowing past us, in an attempt to freeze dry the mud which stuck to our whole bodies.

What the hell would we do, now? We had lost our base, and everything inside it. We were completely on our own. We had no food, no water and no shelter.

The sun was starting to set. We had no idea where we were going to go. With no protection and no car there wasn't anywhere we could go, apart from deeper into the woodland.

I thought back to the events that inevitably brought us to this. The weeks we spent trapped in the apartment. The time we spent at the base. We never thought it at the time, but we were living in luxury.

Okay, so none of us had a fresh home-cooked meal for months. But we had a warm bed to go to each night, and we always had a roof over our heads. The danger of the infected was minimal. Yes, we had a few close calls, but we were easily able to escape.

Looking around the woodland in front of me, I started to appreciate what we had before. I had no idea how we were going to survive our new conditions.

The infected were a bigger threat than ever. But they weren't our only set-back. We would have to work harder than ever, just to stay alive, to survive in the outside world.

None of us knew where our path would take us, or where we would end up. This really was the beginning of the end.

Epilogue

The Sergeant opened his eyes for the first time. The world around him fogged over. He was in a dark place. He looked down to his blood socked uniform; bits of flesh and tissue clung to his body and floated on the deep dark pools of blood around him.

He felt no pain. He glanced around the room; concrete lined the walls and the ground. The long passageway lay out in front of him, prompting him to pull himself up and from the floor and follow the path ahead.

As he stumbled to find his footing, he clung to the wall. With his head resting on the cool concrete he heard faint voices up ahead. As the voices faded into the distance he started to follow, as a new hunger started to build up inside him.

He stayed close to the wall, he moved slowly at first, his legs not quite responding the way he wanted them to. This started to frustrate him, he groaned as he fought to propel himself forward.

After a while his body, now used to the forward motion, started to react a lot quicker. Picking up his pace, he rapidly closed in on the voices. As he pushed on he looked down. Small creatures were scrambling around him, his presence clearly alerting them to a danger of some sorts. This didn't interest him in the slightest.

As he turned the final corner he came face to face with the source of the voices. A man stood in front of him, trying desperately to climb up into a small opening. The Sergeant stopped and stared. The man held some sort of familiarity to the Sergeant, but for as hard as he tried he just couldn't figure out why. He felt his hunger well up inside, this time it was much worse. It coursed through his whole body as he opened his mouth and screeched. Black viscous liquid poured out his mouth as he threw himself desperately, towards the man.

The small creatures gathered beneath him, slowing down his pursuit. He fought his way over to the man, who was now halfway through the crawlspace. Trying desperately to get a hold of the man he reached out to grasp his foot.

He was seconds too late; the man had already broken free. Without hesitation he climbed up into the crawlspace in pursuit of the man. As the light illuminated the exit he saw the man was not alone. Standing before him were seven other figures, all with the same expression. Hearing a rustling from behind him he looked around. Before he had time to react, a solid heavy force came crushing down on him, crushing his skull, and throwing him into permanent darkness.

E Virus
The Diary of a Modern Day Girl
Book 2
The Path of Destruction

Coming Soon

www.facebook.com/jessicawardauthor
Instagram @jesswardauthor
www.jessicaward.info